AFFAIR

TO

DISMEMBER

A Nola Martin Mystery

MARJORIE DARIO

ISBN: 9781796611625

AFFAIR TO DISMEMBER

Edited by Mouse Editing Services

Dedication

This Nola Martin Mystery is dedicated to my father, Alfred Vernon Krohn. He took me camping, hiking, backpacking, sailing, snow skiing, horseback riding, and taught me ballroom dancing when I was young. I spent every teenage summer on his homestead property in Plumas County, California, where we all stayed in the log cabin he had built by hand. A machinist by trade, he taught me how to work with tools, fix things, and so much more that still comes in handy today. My dad was truly a "sailor on horseback" who was born, coincidentally, the same year Jack London died.

Acknowledgements

I'd like to thank my family, friends and readers (too numerous to name) for encouraging me to continue writing. Not easy—especially when life keeps throwing you rotten apples. But, I have learned to toss them aside and keep right on typing. I am also grateful to Peter Mark Roget for publishing his Thesaurus in 1852. Couldn't do it without your help, Pete.

Nola Martin Mysteries

Bad Fortune

Affair to Dismember

Buzz Kill (coming next)

1

The three-legged dog was carrying something in its mouth. From a distance it looked like one of those rubber hands. You know, the kind that novelty shops sell? But I couldn't really tell for sure what it was. The scruffy mutt continued to lope its way past my front yard, seemingly oblivious to its missing right back leg.

I was sitting out on the front veranda of my historic house that I had been in the process of remodeling, while taking a break from my job at the weekly newspaper. I had bought the house not long after moving back to my home town. I was lucky to get the reporter job at the Cider Press to help pay for the renovations.

It was a pleasant late September afternoon in Cider Crossing, considering we had just experienced the hottest, driest summer in quite some time. A lot of plants had died or were suffering, including some of my own. The local botanical society wasn't happy about that, being their fall flower show was coming up in a few days. Entries might be slim, I was afraid.

I took another sip of my pomegranate iced tea, contemplating what my next remodel project should be. It was difficult getting the professional help I needed in this small town, but I had managed to have the kitchen and main bathroom redone with retro touches, and I'd added a second bathroom off the master bedroom. I was still trying to decide what to have done next. Floors? Ceilings? Just then the phone began to ring inside the house.

"Nola, are you there? Pick up, please" I recognized my mother Lillian's voice on the answering machine as I walked through the wide-open French doors.

"Hi, Mom, what's up?"

"Have you seen or heard from Myrtle lately? I mean, you being the society columnist and all, I thought I'd check with you first. She's not answering her phone and no one has seen her out and about. I'm getting a little worried. Oh, my, I wish she belonged to the Up-and-At'em group. We keep close tabs on each other by phoning our assigned person every single morning. But, I know you already know this, dear." She paused to take a breath. "Of course, Myrtle is too stubborn and independent to join us." Another short pause. "Maybe she went to visit Ivy and didn't tell anyone. Someone must be taking care of her cat, I mean . . ."

"No, Mom, I haven't seen her," I interrupted her rambling before she got too wound up. "Have you called Charlie or Blanche? Maybe they know where she is. I haven't heard anything, but I'm thinking she should be back soon to enter her yellow hibiscus in the flower show like she always does. Unless she had a lot of buds drop off this summer, which means she may not have any flowers to show." Now, *I* was rambling. "Anyway, call her son or daughter-in-law. I'm sure she's fine."

After hanging up, I thought of driving by Myrtle's house to see for myself, but I had to return to work, and since the Cider Press newspaper office was within walking distance, I decided to walk over. The community awards dinner would be held in less than two weeks and I needed to review the press kit even though I knew most of the nominees personally. An advantage, or as some might say *disadvantage*, of living in a small town.

I made sure that Flossie, my fur baby, was safely inside the house before I set out on foot. The stray white cat had showed up on my front porch one day, and looked so emaciated that I felt compelled to rescue her. She was so skinny, bringing to mind dental floss, which is how I came up with her name. Of course, after feeding her for a while the name choice was not as obvious anymore. I had her spayed right away to avert any more stray cats roaming around town.

I had vowed never to take in a pet again after our beloved Belgian Malinois, Bruno, had died. My late husband Marty and I had adopted him when he didn't pass muster as a police dog. His original name had been Butch, but we liked the name Bruno much better, for some reason. He was a very loving guard dog (a contradiction, I know) who was diagnosed with a rare bone marrow disease.

But he had succumbed to that ailment before we even had a chance to have him treated at the University of California, Davis, veterinary teaching hospital, which our vet had been arranging. We were both terribly devastated by his loss.

Nevertheless, I had broken my vow when I moved back home to Cider Crossing.

When I first moved back to town, I was talked into adopting Bertie, now *my* cockatoo, when Mother's friend Gertrude passed away. He's pretty easy to deal with, even though he talks a lot. I'm not sure how old he is, but cockatoos can live to be over 60 years old, so he may even outlive me. Gertrude had named him after Bert Parks, and had taught him to sing the first lines of the Miss America theme song, among other tunes and phrases.

So, Flossie, Bertie and I shared a life together after all.

With my key ring in one hand and my outdated flip phone in the other, I made my way the few blocks down the street and unlocked the door into an empty office. The other reporter, Calvin Smythe, must be out on assignment, I thought. And Dora Lightfoot, the part-time office manager, usually took off shortly after noon. Julius Dixon, the editor, was on vacation in Alaska, so it was up to me and Cal to get the weekly edition out in his absence.

The press kit was in Julius' in-box, thanks to Dora's efficient office management. I placed it in my tote bag for later. It was already Wednesday and there was a ton of work to do before the pages were sent to the printer the next day for the Friday edition. I had been working on layout all day and needed to get some copy written. Cal, who had no other life, would probably be working well into the night.

I had decided to work on my column at home. Living alone was another advantage. I could do whatever, whenever. Of course, the downside of being a widow was living alone.

The secondhand police scanner squawked as I was about to grab my tote bag and head out the front door. Something about "body part" caught my attention but the quality of the transmission was poor, as usual. I turned around to concentrate on what the dispatcher was saying.

"Party states . . . dog . . . running around . . . appears . . . hand . . . Sixth and Elm."

I grabbed my tote bag, locked up and made my way to the reported location on foot. Apparently, someone else had spotted the same three-legged dog I had seen earlier, I was willing to bet.

I reached the neighborhood in less than eight minutes, and since I never go on an assignment without my reporter's notebook and digital camera, I was ready for action. There wasn't much going on, however, except for the sudden gathering of onlookers that always occurs whenever several of the town's patrol cars converge at the same time.

The dog had already been caged by Cider Crossing's sole animal control officer, and the hand, which could very well be human, apparently had been placed in a paper bag and was resting on the hood of one of the patrol cars.

In the shade of some oleander bushes, it appeared that the boy who spotted the dog, and maybe his mom, who had probably made the call, were both being interviewed by one of the two police officers on scene—Jeff Frye.

All I learned from the other officer, Jim Bixby, was that they had no perpetrator or crime scene, thus far, and the hand would be sent out to the nearest lab, which wasn't that near. I didn't care to look at it, so I had him describe its appearance.

"Dirty," he said. "Dirt under the fingernails. One finger missing. Pinky finger."

My first thought was it might belong to a vagrant, but the officer assured me they hadn't seen any new drifters about lately, just the usual homeless souls who camped down by the railroad tracks.

"Could you tell if it was real?" I asked.

"Oh, it looks real alright."

"What about male or female?" I couldn't think of any other appropriate questions to ask regarding a body part.

"Nah, too shriveled up. Lab guys will figure that out, though," the officer said as he returned to his patrol car.

Both the cops were pretty sure the dog didn't do it, but he would be incarcerated at the animal shelter anyway. They were taking him in for stray behavior and possible evidence. If the dog knew anything about this, he wasn't talking.

I snapped some photos and took down a few notes. The story would obviously be sensational, but finding out more details could take a few days, at the very least. I was determined to gather more information before the week's edition went to press the next day.

"Thanks, Jimmy and Jeff," I hollered as the officers took off in separate directions. I couldn't help calling them by their first names, considering they went to school with my kids, Amelia and James.

I found myself nine blocks away from home by then, so I trudged off puzzling over possible scenarios. Okay, so the dog came upon a dead body and removed the hand? Unlikely, but, if so, what's a dead body doing lying around in the first place?

Or, could the dog be a grave robber? No, even though the cemetery on the outskirts of town was small, it still had to comply with health and safety regulations. Like body containment, for one. Surely, the dog didn't dig up an entire casket and remove one hand. The hand was dirty, Jeff had said. Like it had been buried in a shallow grave along with its body? Is someone burying corpses in our midst? Nah.

It would be obvious if someone in this small town were missing.

But someone *was* missing. I hurried along, reminding myself to call Mother when I got home to see if she had located Myrtle.

2

The phone was ringing as I unlocked my front door. "They don't know where she is," my mother blurted out frantically before I could even say 'Hello.'

"Well, did they check with Ivy?" I questioned, trying to remain calm and think like a reporter. "I'm sure Ivy would know something."

"Ivy doesn't know where she is, either. But, Charlie didn't seem that worried. He said maybe he knew where she was, but he wouldn't tell me. I don't understand. The only out-of-town trip she ever makes is to visit Ivy and her family in Dowd. Why wouldn't Charlie be concerned? You know what a mama's boy he is, even at his age." Mother sighed, and then picked up where she left off. "Can you investigate this, Nola? Isn't that what reporters are supposed to do?"

"Mom, I'm just a reporter who writes about various people and things in this small community. Investigating missing persons is not part of my job description," I grumbled. "But, I'll drive over to her house tomorrow and have a look around anyway. Do you want me to pick you up?" I decided not to tell her about the hand. She'd be reading about it soon enough.

"No, dear, Nellie Semple is coming over sometime tomorrow to pick up my banana nut bread recipe, so I have to be here waiting for her. You know, she's taken an interest in baking lately. Third recipe she's borrowed this month. Used to be, she hardly ever used her oven to bake anything. Was probably clean as a whistle. It's a good thing mine is self-cleaning, being I use it almost every day. Which reminds me, I need to . . ."

I halted her stream of consciousness with, "Mom, I've got work to do tonight, I'll talk to you tomorrow, okay?" I didn't mean to be rude, but, heaven knows, if I hadn't interrupted her I'd still be on the phone today.

After I fed the pets and picked through a few leftovers for dinner, I sat down to work on my column. But first I did a quick review of the press kit for the community awards event before deciding I needed to set up interviews with each of the nominees. So, I left that task for office work the next day.

It seemed like I'd covered every aspect of this town in a hundred different ways. I was running out of ideas. Fortunately, the town was full of them if you tapped into the grapevine. The most exciting thing to happen lately was when Junior Semple, Nellie's son, had caught himself on fire while dousing his hibachi with gasoline. Inside his garage, no less. He wasn't burned that badly, but he would have been better off if he hadn't gone running down the street. What a stupid thing to do. Good thing Iris Pettis was a few doors down watering her petunias with a garden hose when that happened. She sprayed him down to extinguish the flames. Junior may have been doused, but he still remains stupid.

I did the best I could to keep my column interesting, such as it was. There were always a few births, deaths, weddings, exotic vacations or family reunions to report, but this week's column was turning out to be boring. Maybe it was time for me to retire—again. Let someone else carry on the Cider Crossing tradition. At least our newspaper still had one. Society columns were tossed a long time ago in bigger cities. You had to be a celebrity to get attention nowadays, whether it be positive or negative. Who cared anymore if Mary Smith's pecan pie won a blue ribbon at the county fair? Or the mayor's son won the local spelling bee contest?

I checked my notes and whipped up a few notable items: The Claytons had been to the Grand Canyon and the Moores just got back from the Bahamas. The Bellinis were headed to Italy to attend a relative's wedding. I did my best to be creative and make all their adventures sound interesting. Actually, I wouldn't mind going on an adventure myself. Instead, I'm writing about other people's fun times, I complained, instead of making the most of the rest of my life. Marty and I had often talked about taking a trip to Australia, but I didn't want to go alone.

Column finished, I decided to give Officer Jeff a quick call to see if there was any news on the mysterious hand. He answered his cell phone immediately with "Hey, Nola."

"Hey, Jeff, I was wondering if the hand made it to the lab yet, and when we might be hearing something," I said to get right to the point. I had no idea how long it would take for the lab to obtain any definitive results.

"It's still in transit, as far as I know. We didn't have anyone to drive it over, so someone over in Dowd had to come all the way over to fetch it. Whoa, no dog jokes intended." Right, cop humor, I thought. "He left here about an hour ago, so he should be almost there."

"Well, could you keep me posted, please? If there's any breaking news I want to get it in this next edition," I pleaded.

"Sure thing."

It suddenly hit me that Cal may not know what's been going on, so I disconnected with Jeff and called the office.

"Cider Press, Smythe here." He always pronounced his last name in the British fashion, with a long "I" and soft "th" sound.

"Cal, it's Nola. How's it going? I've been working on my column at home."

"She's coming along. Got the front page layout almost completed. Could use some help, Nola," he reproved.

I ignored that barb by saying, "Well, we might want to leave room for a breaking story. Seems a body part was discovered over at Sixth and Elm and it appeared to be a human hand."

"Sixth and Elm? In someone's yard?"

"Actually, it was traveling all over town before that. A three-legged dog was running around with it in its mouth. So, who knows where it came from? Anyway, it's on its way to the lab over in Dowd, but we probably won't find out anything for a few days."

"Interesting. Okay, I'll save room for it, time permitting. We only have one more day 'til she goes to bed, you know."

"I *do* know, Cal. Just because I have blonde hair doesn't make me dumb. Besides, I'll be worthless if *I'm* the one that doesn't go to bed soon. Good night."

I didn't feel sleepy yet, so I went into the parlor and turned on the TV. I flipped through the channels until I found something to watch. A short time later I started to become groggy, so I decided to hit the sack like I said I would.

3

The next morning, as I was about to leave for the office, the house phone snagged me again. I almost didn't answer it, since I had nothing yet to report to my mother. But my curiosity got the better of me, so I picked up the receiver.

"Thought you'd like to know that another body part has turned up. This time it's a foot," said Officer Jeff before I spoke one word.

"Yikes! Where was it found? Another dog toy?" I couldn't help borrowing his sense of humor.

"No, some kids were digging around down by the railroad tracks and found it. Bet it scared the daylights out of them. We've got a volunteer team over there right now searching for the rest of the body. Most likely it's related to the hand, I'm guessing. I'll keep you posted." That said, he abruptly hung up, leaving me to wonder.

I was afraid it would turn out to belong to someone I knew, so I decided to swing by Myrtle's house on my way to the office.

I drove in a zigzag pattern through the older residential section of town. A lot of the dwellings had been rejuvenated, but some hadn't seen a coat of paint or a new roof in years. Others had been demolished. The town was almost one hundred years old and it was amazing that any of the original homes were still standing.

Cider Crossing had been a bustling town many years ago, thanks to the railroad, but when the interstate bypass opened and passenger train service was curtailed, it seemed the historic settlement simply froze in time—and then it began to melt away.

Established at the intersection of two wagon trails, the crossing became noted for its apple cider stand erected by the owner of a nearby apple orchard, hence the name. That crossing is now a parking lot next to the only bank in town along the only main street in town. And, unfortunately, the train doesn't stop here anymore.

I waved at Iris Pettis as I passed by her lovely home. Iris, as usual, was working in her garden. There were healthy-looking flowers and plants of every variety and color in her yard. The woman seemed to devote all her time to that pursuit, since her husband, Bertrand, had recently passed away. She was definitely spending a lot of time at it, and it showed. I had even seen her out there working away long after dark.

I pulled into Myrtle's driveway. It was another lovely older home that had been updated to accommodate modern conveniences, like cars. Letting myself through the front gate I hopped up the steps to the porch. Ceramic tiles spelled out "Maxwell" over the entry door. I was about to knock when I heard meowing sounds coming from inside.

I moved over to the nearest window and peered inside. Nothing was in disarray, but I couldn't see a cat. Returning to the door, I decided to ring the bell instead. The chimes sounded and the cat meowed, but Myrtle didn't answer.

Walking around toward the back of the house, I noticed Myrtle's prize hibiscus plants were in dire need of a drink of water. I grabbed a nearby hose and flooded the wells beneath each plant. Surely, whoever is taking care of the cat should also be doing the watering, I thought. That is, if Myrtle actually did go out of town.

It was when I was turning off the water faucet that I sniffed a peculiar burning smell coming from the slightly open kitchen window. I tried to look in, but the window was too high up.

"Phew, what *is* that?" I said aloud.

As I was coming back down the side of the house, a car was pulling up in front. Charlie Maxwell got out of his luxury sedan and gave me a perplexed look over the top of his car.

"What are you doing here, Nola? Is my mother home?"

"Apparently not. The cat is crying, the hibiscus plants are dying and there's an awful odor wafting from the kitchen. Who's taking care of things here?"

"Well, I guess I am. Mom musta forgot to let me know she was going out of town. She's forgetful like that sometimes."

He didn't seem that concerned. I, on the other hand, thought it all a little strange.

"She never mentioned anything when we had her over for dinner last week," he continued.

"So, you don't know when she left or where she is?" I was perplexed.

"Not really. But she's done this before, darn her. I told her not to go."

"So, you *do* know where she is? I'm confused."

"No, I don't know for sure, but she's not at Ivy's, so there's only one other place she might be." He sounded dejected.

"And where would that be?" I was running out of patience.

"I don't want to say. But she should be back soon. She's usually only gone for a few days each time."

"Okay, fine. But you need to get in there and check on the cat. Also, find out what is causing that awful smell." I pinched my nose shut.

He got out his keys and I followed him, uninvited, into the house. The smell had permeated every room. In the kitchen we found a burnt pan on the stove and two exploded eggs that had landed on the floor next to the cat's feeding dishes. The eggs were way past hard boiled and the cat's bowls were empty.

Grabbing a hot pad off of a hook near the stove, I turned off the burner, picked up the pan and dropped it in the sink under running water.

"What the . . .?" I shouted through a cloud of hissing steam. Charlie just stood there.

"I told you she was forgetful," was all he could say.

"Get the cat some food and water while I open some windows," I said.

I ran around the house shoving up some stubborn, single-hung wooden windows, and then returned to the kitchen.

"If you ask me, it looks like she left in a hurry—to say the least," I said, stating the obvious.

The cat came running in as Charlie put away the bag of cat food and then turned to me. His balding head had taken on a pinkish tinge. In measured syllables he uttered, "No-la, this is real-ly none of your biz-ness."

"Well, actually, Charlie, it is. You see, as a society columnist I like to keep up on everyone's comings and goings. I mean, if your mom went somewhere exciting I'd like to report it. That's why it's okay to tell me where she is so she'll get her name in the paper. So, where do you think . . . ?"

"Nola, stop! If Mom wants to talk to you when she gets back, that's up to her. I wouldn't tell you where she was, even if I knew."

"So, you don't know where she is? Why do you keep changing your story, Charlie?"

"It's time for you to leave, Nola. I'll lock up."

I was being dismissed, so I walked back out to my car.

As I drove away, I could see that Myrtle's open mailbox appeared to be filled to the brim.

Driving toward the office it occurred to me that if Charlie wouldn't talk to me, then maybe his wife, Blanche, would. She was always primed and ready to dish the dirt on her mother-in-law. Not that there was any dirt to dish.

Myrtle and Ernie had led an exemplary life. Ernie ran his retail business and Myrtle kept the house spotless while rearing two children. No one ever said anything bad about any of them. Of course, Myrtle had spoiled Charlie rotten before Ivy came along. It always seemed Charlie was jealous of his baby sister, which is probably why Myrtle continued to spoil him. Either that or he was simply out of control by that time. Charlie was ten when Ivy was born.

I thought maybe when Charlie moved out, and started his own insurance business, he would finally begin to mature. But all the signs were still there of a doting mother and a dependent son. Some things never change. Of course, when he married Blanche, who is a few years younger than Ivy, people thought this would turn him into a man. Little did they know that Blanche, with her belittling ways, only helped to further emasculate him. Blanche partnered her real estate and property management business with Charlie's so they could share an office, but everyone knew who the real boss was.

* * * *

Cal wasn't in the office when I got there. Dora was on the phone, two colorful chopsticks stabbed precariously into a large wad of black hair at the back of her head.

"Cal say where he was going?" I asked Dora as soon as she hung up.

"Nope. He must have heard something on the scanner 'cause he grabbed his equipment and ran out the door," she answered. "I can't understand all that garbled radio talk, so I have no idea what the big hurry was."

I figured I'd find out what Cal was up to soon enough. Although I had good intentions of laying out my column, I decided it could wait. Instead, I called Blanche at her office and she agreed to meet me for lunch, after her weekly manicure.

Cal came in right after I hung up the phone, so I started to fill him in on the latest body part discovery. He'd already heard. In fact, he said he had just come from the site.

"Did they find the rest of the body?" I inquired, feeling rather ghoulish.

"Nothing. And I watched them dig for quite a while. Took some photos. Meanwhile, the foot's gone off to Dowd. Hopefully, we'll hear something soon."

"I'll keep checking," I offered.

"I can't decide whether to run what we know so far or to hold off 'til we have the complete story. I've got to shoot the pages to the printer by four this afternoon, and there's not a lot of room left. I'd have to pull something. Plus, if the other media catch wind of this they'll try to scoop us. Jeez. Maybe we'd better wait. What do you think, Nola?"

"I think you're right. We should hold off with the article as long as we can."

"Okay, let's wait," Cal agreed.

I followed him over to his desk. "Good golly. Two body parts in two days. Coincidence? They've gotta be from the same person, don't you think?"

"I don't know what to think, except it's pretty darn exciting for such a small town. And great for the newspaper." Cal professed. "Like Julius always says, 'If it bleeds, it leads.' I hope we can run something before the wires catch wind of it. Speaking of wind, I've got to get busy and write up the town hall meeting story. A lot of hot air, as usual."

Back at my computer, I cut and pasted my column into its reserved space on page three and it fit perfectly. I proofread it one more time, and then typed up some community briefs. The elementary school was having a bake sale and a yoga class was starting soon at one of the local churches. Finally it was time to meet Blanche at Lulu's Café.

"I'll be back," I hollered at Cal as I went out the door.

* * * *

Blanche was sitting at a table facing the door when I showed up. She waved a newly manicured hand at me. Her perfectly coiffed blonde hair didn't move an inch. Neither did her silicone cleavage.

Trying not to feel self-conscious about needing my hair and nails done, too, I greeted her like the friend she really wasn't as I pulled out the chair to her left. We quickly ordered from the menu, and then I got right down to my reason for calling her.

"So, Charlie and I were checking on Myrtle this morning and it looks like she left in a hurry," I jumped in. "When's the last time you saw her?"

"At least a week ago. Mom's like that. She gets a bee in her bonnet and off she goes."

"Doesn't she usually tell you where she's going and when she'll be back? I mean, someone's gotta take care of the house and all."

"Not always. It depends on how long she'll be gone. Of course, if she's where I think she is, then that could vary."

The waitress had brought out our raspberry iced teas.

I took a sip as I switched into my nonchalant mode. "And where would that be?"

"Well, Charlie doesn't know that I know this, but . . . I think Mom's got herself a boyfriend in another town. Charlie's real upset about that, which is why I can't talk to him about it. But Mom, herself, hinted about this man to me a while ago. I think it's someone she went to high school with, but since it's all so hush-hush I'm thinking he must be married. Don't you think? I mean, why would she be so secretive if he wasn't?"

"That's outrageous! Myrtle, at her age?" I said, feigning shock. "Of course, if they've known each other all this time . . . how long do you think this has been going on? Your father-in-law's been dead almost ten years, right?"

"I think so. That was before my time . . . before Charlie and I met.

"Why do you think Charlie is so upset about this? Because his mom's seeing a married man?" I was goading her for more information.

"No, because Charlie wants *all* of his mother's attention. Plain old jealousy is what I think. He's insanely jealous. He wants her all to himself. If you ask me, he should be more worried about some old guy coming in and robbing him of his inheritance. If Mom got married again, Charlie could end up with nothing, and I'd be pissed. Myrtle is sitting on a fortune because she's so tight with her money. It would be a good thing if this guy's already married, or Charlie could end up with a stepdad. Of course, the man could always get a divorce or his wife could die, but . . ."

Our food was served and Blanche began picking at her taco salad.

I picked up the conversation. "So, you think Myrtle is spending time with this married man in another town? Do you know where that is or what his name is?"

"No, she didn't give me any details. Like I said, she only hinted around about him. But I noticed she had dug out her old high school year book one day and one of the pages is bookmarked. There's an autographed photo of a guy named George something-or-other on that page. Nice looking, but he'd be Myrtle's age now, I had to remind myself, you know, balding, pot belly . . ."

"What year was that book? Do you remember?" I had the tiniest seed of an idea germinating.

"Nah. Wasn't paying that much attention. Maybe Charlie would know, but it's such a touchy subject with him. I feel it's best to let that one go."

"Oh, sure, I was simply curious, that's all," I conceded as I took in a forkful of my Caesar salad.

"Personally, I'm glad she's gone . . . out of town, I mean. When she's here she's always poking her nose into our business, personal and otherwise. I can't stand her dropping by the house or office without calling first. It's really annoying. Sometimes I wish she would go away and not come back. But then Charlie would be hell to live with. How about you? Do you have a mother-in-law?" Blanche asked.

"Not any more. She died a few years before my husband did. My mother still lives here in town, however, and she's a bit of a handful herself," I commiserated.

I really wanted to know more about this mystery man Myrtle might be involved with, but Blanche, tiring of her salad, looked about ready to leave. She was brushing taco crumbs from her pale green linen miniskirt. I took a few more bites of my salad and crunched on the croutons.

"I've gotta get back to the office, Nola. It was nice seeing you," Blanche announced before I could get out one last question between lettuce and croutons. I wanted to ask her if she had heard about the two gruesome discoveries.

Right then my cell phone sounded the office ringtone, and Cal informed me that a *third* body part had turned up. When I flipped my cell shut, Blanche was gone.

4

As I drove by the Maxwell's office building, I could see there were no cars in the tiny front parking lot. Didn't Blanche say she was heading back to the office? Hmmm. She must be out showing a property, but where's Charlie's car? And why do I care? Must be reporter's syndrome, I rationalized. All unusual behavior becomes curious and suspicious in the journalist's world.

One block later, I arrived at the Cider Press office. Cal was waiting for me in the open doorway. Exasperation was written all over his face.

"This story is growing fast but we're running out of time," he complained.

"Okay. Calm down and fill me in on the latest. Where'd this one turn up and which body part is it?"

"It's a finger, but it wasn't found at the same site as the foot," Cal continued. "This one was lying in plain sight atop the historical marker in the community park at the edge of town. A couple of tourists from Germany found it and went straight to the police station with the finger in a 35 millimeter film canister. I happened to be over there checking the log sheet when I overheard what they were trying to say, only in broken English. My little bit of German picked up *gefunden*, the word for "found," when I realized they were also saying *finger*, which is the same in both languages, by the way. Elsa Mae, at the counter, thought they were trying to drop off their film for processing.

"Anyway, Captain Peachtree had them take him back to the marker and show him exactly where it was. I followed them over there and they pointed to the top of the marker. There didn't appear to be any blood around so I don't know if they'll call the crime scene guys over to process or not."

It was the most words I'd heard Cal speak that fast in one breath, ever. "So, it might be the missing finger from the hand, but how did it get on top of the marker? It's, what, four feet high?" I offered my estimate.

"Approximately. Obviously, the dog didn't put it there," Cal snickered. "They're thinking maybe some kids found it and put it up there as a joke. Some joke, huh?"

"Well, I'll talk to Jeff or Jim later and see if the lab's starting to match up all these gruesome pieces. Meanwhile, we've got final layout to do, right?" I turned and headed toward my desk.

I could tell Cal was glad I was there to help as he began assigning me the pages that needed attention.

I arranged the ads and checked all the "jumps" to and from other pages, all the while wondering what the heck was going on in this sleepy little town and whose body parts were being strewn all over the place.

Since we hadn't gleaned any more information about the body parts, Cal was forced to go ahead and put the paper to bed. We both were hoping that we'd have all we needed by the next edition.

I worked on a few more housekeeping tasks and started preparing my itinerary for the week ahead.

Before I knew it, it was after six, so I told Cal I was heading home and would be back bright and early in the morning. He grumbled his usual parting words from behind his partition as I was going out the door, but I kept right on moving. I always try not to engage Cal when he is in one of his grumpy moods.

As I pulled out of the parking lot, something made me turn right instead of left and I found myself heading back to Myrtle's house. George, her mystery man, had been taunting me to find out more about him. Why? Certainly not for prurient reasons. I somehow felt if I could find him I could also find Myrtle. That high school yearbook would be the first place to start. I wasn't sure how I would get into the house, but I'd find a way. I've done it before, I reminded myself.

I parked a few doors down and ducked into the driveway, hoping the fading twilight would provide enough cover so the neighbors, or anyone driving by, wouldn't see me.

Creeping around the back of the house, I noticed one of the back windows had not been shut all the way. Thank you, Charlie. I found an old Seeger's Apples crate, upended it, and hoped it would hold my weight while I boosted myself through the window. Good thing Myrtle didn't like the look of solar screens on her house. And good thing I wore pants to work that day.

I had to struggle to get the window up, but once inside I decided to close it all the way. I could exit through the side kitchen door, I thought.

I made my way to the parlor which had a built-in book case. I switched on a small table lamp away from the window. It took me a while to find the yearbooks since they were skinny back then and had nothing written on the spine. There were three. Since Blanche didn't recall the year, I had to look at all of them. There didn't seem to be a bookmark like she said.

Flipping through each volume, I found several young men named George, all with unsigned photos, and I was becoming confused, not trusting Blanche's recollection.

One photo that caught my eye was of a stiffly-posed scholastic society. I hardly recognized any of the members until I read the caption and noted Myrtle Crenshaw and Winifred Goodman. Must be the same Myrtle and Winnie I know, I thought. Although the hairdos were outdated, I could still see a resemblance.

At the bottom of the page was a photo of the chess club. All boys—except for a plain-looking Florence Halladay. She appeared frumpy, even back then. A few pages later I found a better photo of Myrtle holding her scholastic achievement award of the year. Yep, that was her alright.

Finally, I turned a page and a slender pink ribbon marked the spot. Gregory, not George, for heaven's sake. Jeez, Blanche, are you that careless with your real estate clients' names?

Gregory smiled pleasantly at me from the page. His hair was neatly parted and slicked down. He was nondescript, except for a mole to the right of his mouth. His cramped signature was preceded by "Love Always."

Gregory Allen Goldberg. I'm coming to find you, Greg. How hard could that be? I returned the books to the shelf, switched off the lamp, and then headed back to the kitchen.

Leaving by the kitchen door, which turned out not to be locked after all, I removed the crate from beneath the window and "stealthed" my way back to my car, under cover of darkness this time.

As soon as I got back home I sat down at my computer and started running a people search. It took me three minutes and a few seconds to find Gregory. Of all things, he was shown as living in Dowd, but his address and phone number were not posted. The newspaper office had a Dowd phone book, however.

I grabbed something to eat, fed the pets, and then headed over to the office, hoping Cal would be gone by then.

Arriving on foot, I noticed the back office lights were on for security purposes, but no cars were parked out front, so I let myself in and locked the door behind me.

In the dimly lit front office I found the Dowd phone book and Gregory's home number and address. So, he wasn't trying to hide from anyone, it appeared. I scribbled his number down on a pink sticky note. Now, all I had to do was call him. And say what? Okay, I needed a plan, a script, something to give me a reason for calling.

It only took me a few minutes for me to come up with a reporter's angle of writing a piece called "Where Are They Now?" about graduates of Cider

Crossing High. I was sure I could pull it off and also fit in a question or two about Myrtle.

I was about to lift the receiver when I was startled by the unmistakable sound of breaking glass. I froze. Minutes passed without another sound. Since the office didn't have an alarm, help would *not* be on the way. I steeled my nerves to have a look around the corner into the editor's office.

The front picture window was shattered and shards of glass covered the heaping mess that Julius called his desk. I turned and headed into the back room to call the police. I was told a squad car was on the way.

5

"Nola, are you in there?" Jeff's voice came through the broken window.

"Back here," I returned. "Is it safe to come out?" That was fast. How did he get here so quickly? I wondered.

"Yeah. I was just coming around the corner when I heard the glass breaking. Can you let me in, Nola?"

I turned on all the lights and unlocked the front door to let him in.

"How did you know I was in here? There are no cars in the parking lot."

"Call came in just as I was getting out of the car. Are you alright?"

"A little shaken is all. But it could have been Cal who made the call. I'm sorry, I'm babbling, aren't I?"

"Cal doesn't walk to work. Now let's have a look around. Jim should be out there checking for suspicious persons fleeing the scene."

Flashlight in hand, Jeff swept it around Julius' office until he landed on an object tied with string sitting on the floor. A rock. With a piece of paper wrapped around it. How original.

Donning latex gloves from his back pocket, Jeff carefully untied the rock and opened the note.

"BACK OFF" had been boldly written with a black marker.

"Do you know what this could be about?" Jeff asked while holding the warning note up to me with one hand.

I looked at Jeff without registering his question. The sticky note was still in my hand. "I'm sorry, what?"

"Does this make any sense to you? Why would someone do this? C'mon, Nola, get it into reporter gear."

"Oh, yeah, right." Maybe there was a connection to those body parts, I thought, but maybe not. I wasn't sure what was going on. My head was spinning. Who knew about the body parts investigation, or that I had been digging around about Myrtle's disappearance? Was there, in fact, a connection between the two?

"Perhaps some disgruntled reader," I finally replied. "Any news on those three body parts yet?"

"Oh, yeah, I heard about the finger. Apparently, it's on its way to Dowd also. Haven't heard anything else, but I'd be surprised if they weren't all from the same body."

I cleared my throat. "I think you should know that Myrtle Maxwell is missing, because I don't think her family has reported it." I couldn't tell him about the Gregory "discovery" because I had obtained that information by sort of breaking and entering, so I pointed him to Charlie. "Maybe you should talk to

Charlie," I said. "I'm sure he knows something he's not telling."

"Fine. But what about this warning note?" Jeff, like a hound dog, was back on the scent.

"I don't know what could have prompted this," I answered, finally taking a stance.

"Is there anything controversial that you reporters are working on?" Jeff was staring me down.

"Controversial? In this town?" I laughed, but Jeff didn't. "No, absolutely not," I soberly continued when Jeff didn't break his stare.

"Well, you're gonna have to call Harold at home to come over and board this place up. He can replace the window tomorrow. Meanwhile, I don't want you in here alone."

Through the shattered glass, we saw Cal drive up. "What the heck?" he said as he emerged from his car. We could hear him clearly through the broken window.

Cal, camera bag hanging on his shoulder, stood outside taking in the destruction as we talked through the hole in the pane.

"Nola can fill you in, Cal. I've gotta get back on the street. I'm taking this parting gift with me," Jeff said as he carried the rock out to his patrol car. "Call Harold," he ordered as he opened the car door.

"I have to call Harold," I said as I headed for the phone.

"Wait a minute, what's this all about?" Cal was still in the dark, literally.

"Oh, probably some unhappy reader who threw a rock through the window with a note attached advising us to back off."

"Back off? From what?" Cal was as puzzled as I was as he made his way through the front door.

"That's what we need to figure out," I concluded.

Harold Raymond showed up about 15 minutes after I called him. His bald head, due to chemotherapy, was covered by a navy blue knit cap. As sick as he was, he appeared to be fine.

"How are you feeling, Harold?" I inquired.

"Pretty good, actually. Done with the chemo," he said, and then changed the subject. "Now, let me get to work or we'll be here all night."

Harold installed the temporary plywood and promised to return first thing in the morning with the plate glass needed to repair the window. By then it was almost nine. Cal and I had tired of brainstorming possible suspects, concluding nothing substantial, so he drove me home.

He dropped me off in front. I grabbed the mail out of my curbside mail box and went inside.

My blinking message light caught my eye at the same time I realized I had yet to call Gregory. Since it was almost nine, I decided to make the call without wasting the time to retrieve the pending message.

6

Gregory answered after three rings. I introduced myself, apologized for the late hour and he agreed to the interview for the article I was supposedly writing on former students. He said his wife, who was not well, had already gone to bed so he would have to talk softly. Married man, exactly as Blanche had suspected.

"Call me Buddy. That's my nickname from high school," Greg said before I could get started.

"So, what did you do right out of high school, Buddy?" Ascending chronologically seemed the simplest approach on the fly.

"Well, I couldn't afford college, so I came to Dowd to work as a clerk in my uncle's law office. I wanted to make enough money to marry my high school sweetheart. But then I got drafted right away at the escalation of the Vietnam War. I assumed the army would put me in an office somewhere stateside, based on my job description, but I was assigned to a supply unit on Okinawa instead. Never saw combat, not that I wanted to. I was anxious to get back home and get on with my life. But I have nothing but admiration for my fellow soldiers who fought in battle," he quickly added. "Unfortunately, my girlfriend married someone else before I was discharged back to the States."

This interview was turning out to be a piece of cake. Usually I had to work at drawing people out. Buddy was handing me a hefty slice covered in butter cream frosting on a Mikasa plate. I couldn't appear too anxious about the girlfriend, however, so I skirted that subject with the next question.

"I'm sorry to hear that. So, did you return to your job at the law office?"

"Yes. And I was able to work my way through college and become an attorney myself. Along the way I met Greta and we have been married ever since," Greg concluded with an air of satisfaction.

I sensed the next question would be touchy. "Did you ever have any further contact with your old girlfriend . . . what did you say her name was?"

"No," he hesitated, "Why do you ask?"

"Oh, she might be on my list of interviews, that's all."

"Her name is Myrtle. . . uh. . . *was* Myrtle Crenshaw. Married Ernie Maxwell. Haven't seen her in years," he hurriedly added.

Aha, there it was. But I wasn't convinced he was telling the truth. "Well, are there any other details or comments you'd like included in the article?"

"Not really." There was a moment of silence, and then he added, "True love never dies, you know." Buddy had obviously veered off down another path.

"Excuse me?"

"Never mind. I must hang up now. It was nice talking with you. When did you say the article will appear?"

"I'm not sure. Soon," I lied. "Thank you for your time."

He hung up first, and that was it. I was left wondering if I should have probed deeper about his relationship with Myrtle. Of course, he wasn't about to bare his soul to a total stranger. But what if he was told Myrtle was missing? Would he be more forthcoming? I made a mental note to call him back if Myrtle didn't turn up soon.

The message light was still urging me to find out who called. It was Mother, of course. She was frantic because she had heard the body parts rumors. Apparently, word had spread all over town. *Then what the heck do we need a newspaper for?* I asked myself.

Lillian's last words on the machine were, "Nola, I have a bad feeling about this. Call me as soon as you get this message. I don't care how late it is."

Since I honestly just now got her message, and it was, indeed, late by her standards, I decided to be a good daughter and obey my mother.

"What if it's someone we know, Nola?" she cried out as soon as she answered the phone.

I was praying that Myrtle would return home the next day, so that Mother could rest assured it wasn't her friend.

"Mom, we don't know anything for sure yet. The police are working on it and I can't really talk about it right now. Now get some sleep. You're going to get sick if you don't stop worrying." I tried to assuage her fears as mine kept mounting. Role reversal in action.

Heaven forbid she finds out about the rock through the window incident, I thought.

As it turned out, Myrtle did not return home the next day.

7

I always chuckle when I drive past Ernie's Liquor Store on Main Street. It is located in an adjoining building to the right of Bert's Butcher Shop. That's what makes me laugh. Bert and Ernie. Of course, both businesses were established long before Jim Henson's Muppets were born. Little did those two enterprising young businessmen know when they hung up their signs how prophetic they would become. They had opened their shops around the same time back in the late Sixties. Ernie's was still thriving, even though he had been gone for some time. Myrtle, his widow, lived off the profits of alcohol and tobacco sales. Although lately the store was becoming more of the convenience variety, with the addition of a dairy case and some canned foods.

Bert's, on the other hand, had closed down immediately after his recent death. The old-fashioned butcher shop had long been a hold out after the supermarket opened at the other end of town. But it was all Bert knew how to do, so he persisted right up until the day he died. For some reason, Iris wouldn't let go of it either. It was all she had also, since she and

Bert never had any children. So, she continued to pay the utilities, kept the sign up and wouldn't entertain any offers from prospective buyers. Sometimes it's hard to let go. I know all about that, I've been there.

The reason I moved back to my home town from up north had to do with letting go. My husband, Samuel "Marty" Martin, was a police officer who had been killed in the line of duty. Not long after that, I had moved into our retirement cabin in the foothills, having retired early from government service. I soon found it wasn't as blissful as I had envisioned, not having Marty there to share it with me, so I moved down south to my home town to be closer to my widowed mother. My dad, who had been an engineer for the railroad, had left her a tidy widow's pension. She was well taken care of, but I wanted to spend more time with her.

Right away, I bought a grand old lady of a house who was in need of tender loving care and went to work part time at the local newspaper so I could supplement my retirement income while I took care of some repairs and remodeling projects.

I let go. But it still hurt.

I was on my way that morning to the botanical society's clubhouse which was housed in an historic Victorian-style cottage. The judging of the fall flower show was to be held the next day, but some of the entrants would be setting up their displays early. Since the winners wouldn't be announced until the following week, I wanted to snap some early photos in case I ran out of time.

Florence Halladay was scurrying about straightening table coverings and making sure each entrant was properly recorded. The most avid of the society's members, Florence was extremely competitive when it came to roses, rhododendron and such. She was also quite nitpicky and tended to rub people the wrong way, which could explain why she never married. People called her The Old Maid behind her back.

Myrtle and Florence had been long-time rivals at every flower show. Myrtle often won in her category, which made Florence furious. Nobody knew what exactly had started the rivalry, but it had been going on for as long as anybody could remember. The prize money could have something to do with it. Florence could definitely use the money, whereas Myrtle was already well off and only competed for the glory.

Flitting from table to table like a butterfly, Florence was being difficult to net, but I finally got her attention. I told her I needed a copy of the final entrant list as soon as possible. They were still allowing last minute entries, she said, so it may not be ready until the next day.

"Do you know what categories Myrtle Maxwell is entering this time?" I couldn't help needling her.

"No, and I don't care," Florence snorted. "It's getting late, so maybe she won't enter anything. But then again, I don't talk to her, so I wouldn't know." And with that she flitted off again.

I turned around and took a few photos of Winifred Blankenship arranging an abundant assortment of chrysanthemums in a crystal vase. The purples and yellows were breathtaking and the shots would certainly warrant being produced in color.

"Winnie, those mums are gorgeous," I said as I approached her.

"Why, thank you, Nola," she replied with a big smile. "Aren't they heavenly?"

"I understand Myrtle hasn't registered her entries yet. Do you know anything about that?"

"Why, no, I don't. Have you talked to Florence?"

"Well, yes, but you know how Florence's attitude is toward Myrtle. She wasn't much help."

"I haven't been that fond of her either . . . Myrtle, that is. Not since high school. But I've probably spent more time with her lately than in the last fifty-some years. Seems she wanted to be my friend after all. We ran into each other at the grocery store last year and have kept in touch ever since. I usually see her out and about, too. Come to think of it, though, I haven't seen her in over a week now. Strange," she ended abruptly.

"Strange, how?" I asked.

"Well, she never misses a flower show and is usually one of the first ones here to set up. Of course, maybe she doesn't trust Florence," Winnie hinted.

"Oh? Why is that?"

"Well, I heard Florence threatened to ruin Myrtle's display at the spring show. But that's hearsay, like I said," she snickered. "This competition can become vicious for some people, you know. All over a few hundred dollars in prize money. I'm glad I'm not like that. Of course, I'm well taken care of like Myrtle is, but Florence, well, you know . . ." she sniffed. With the remark still hanging in the floral-scented air, she moved over to a cardboard box, scooped up another batch of flowers and held them to her ample bosom, leaving me to ponder over her remarks.

I spotted Olive Quigley arriving, so I made my way in her direction. She was clutching a small vase of rose buds. The pinks and reds matched the paisley scarf on her head.

"Hi, Olive, how are you feeling?" I greeted her.

"Oh, I'm almost done with that chemo stuff and starting to feel a lot better, thank you." She set the vase down on a nearby table and began to fill out her entry form.

I followed her over there. "That makes four people in Cider Crossing currently undergoing chemotherapy that I know of. Let's see . . . you, Harold, Nellie and Archie."

"That's right," Olive replied. "It's so nice of Cecil, I mean Doctor Barber, to shuttle all of us over to Dowd for our treatments. He's been a godsend. Good thing he's semi-retired and has the time to help out. I guess he doesn't have much else to do since his wife died."

"Yes, that is nice of him," I agreed. "Your rosebuds are lovely, Olive," I said, changing the subject. "I'm sure you'll win something. Do you know if Myrtle will be entering her hibiscus this time?"

"Why, thank you, Nola. Of course, I could never compete with Iris Pettis and her roses, but I like to participate anyway. You know, I haven't seen Myrtle in a while. I figured she was busy coaxing her plants to bloom before the show."

An enormous bush of yellow roses was coming through the doorway toted by Archie Tanner, who was also huge. Iris was right behind him.

"Set it over there, Archie," Iris gestured to a corner of the room. "And thank you for helping me get it here."

"No problem, Iris," Archie grunted as he placed the heavy pot down on the floor. He seemed to be doing quite well, considering. His bald head and protruding belly belied the fact that he was ill because he'd looked like that for years.

Iris had second thoughts. "No, maybe you'd better put it up on the table, Archie. I'm afraid I won't be able to lift it later."

Without grumbling, Archie bent down a second time.

"So, Archie, are you entering anything in the show?" Iris asked. "We rarely have men in competition."

He turned to Iris after placing the pot on the table. "Me? I don't do flower shows," he said while brushing his hands clean.

"Oh? I could have sworn I saw you buying one of those grow light things at Peterson's Hardware a few months back," Iris said.

"Ha! I wouldn't be caught dead playing with pansies," Archie chuckled and headed toward the door.

"You could always enter a vegetable plant. We know how you love to eat," Iris insulted.

Florence rushed over to Iris, entry form and pen in hand. "Iris! I thought maybe you weren't showing this year. My, my, what a large entry," she said as she eyed the rose bush.

"I know, Florence. I haven't had time to prune my roses to stimulate blooms so I'm entering a whole bush. Seems that going through Bert's things is taking me more time than I thought it would. Bert wasn't a pack rat, but he did hold on to some stuff. I mean, stuff from fifty years ago? What did he need to keep all that for? Just makes more work for me," she sniffed.

I had been standing nearby scratching out some notes and listening to every word. "Archie? Can I talk to you a sec?" I hollered.

"Sure, Nola," he said as he came to a stop.

I put my notepad away. "Have you seen Myrtle Maxwell lately?"

"No, can't say that I have. Why?"

"Oh, nothing, I was wondering if she was going to enter the contest, that's all."

"Well, if I see her I'll tell her she better get on down here," Archie assured. "I'd best be going now. It's time for my nap," he chuckled and walked off.

Camera in hand, I walked over to Iris' rose bush and started snapping away. I stopped to sniff. The bright yellow flowers were in various stages of development and gave off a slight citrus scent. I took out my notepad to begin writing down which photos belonged to which entrants when Iris came back from completing her paperwork.

"Have you heard from Myrtle lately?" I asked Iris.

"No, but she'll turn up . . . she always does," she mumbled as she turned toward her rose bush. "Like a bad penny, as they say," she added under her breath.

Not knowing how to take that, I changed the subject. "Why the whole bush, Iris, and not a bouquet of cut flowers?" I asked.

"This bush is so beautiful, if I may say so myself, that I didn't want to cut into it. So, I decided to enter the live plant category this season. Dug it up and repotted yesterday so it could get used to the container. Then, knowing it was too heavy for me get it here by myself, I called Archie."

"What's it called? I mean, what's the common name for this rose bush?" I asked.

"Lemon Zest, of course," Iris answered in her uppity fashion.

"Well, that explains the citrus smell," I commented tactfully as I wrote down the name on my notepad.

8

Rather than head back into the office, I decided I'd better check in on Mother.

Lillian Kendall was a strong woman, but lately she seemed to get flustered easily. I used to fool myself into thinking she never seemed to age—but since my father passed away, I could see that she had. She was becoming forgetful and often repeated herself.

I tried to pass these quirks off as common to everyone, even me, but the truth was she was growing older and I needed to face the fact that she wouldn't always be around.

Driving across town, I happened to pass by one of Blanche's real estate listings. A quaint cream-colored cottage on Birch Street. The "For Sale" sign was swinging in the breeze. Blanche's car was parked at the curb. She must be showing the property, I thought.

An empty patrol car was parked further down in front of a vacant lot on the corner. I was thinking I should pull over and see if there was anything newsworthy going on when I glanced in my side view mirror and saw Blanche and Jeff coming out of the house that was for sale. They embraced before she got in her car and he headed down the street toward his police vehicle. Embarrassed by what I had just witnessed, I rapidly turned the corner.

What on earth was that all about? I didn't want to jump to any conclusions, but what possible explanation could there be, other than a little hanky-panky going on. No, they're both married and she has at least ten years on him. Of course not. But then again . . .

I found myself having to take an alternate route to my mother's house, all the while intrigued by what I had seen. Maybe that's how Jeff came to arrive at the scene of the rock-throwing incident so fast. Were they also fooling around in Blanche's office after hours? My wild imagination was chomping at the bit.

Okay, just because there was no romance in my life, I told myself, I shouldn't be assuming everyone else had something going on. I forced myself to rein it in as I pulled up in front of Mother's house.

Knocking on the screen door before letting myself in, I called out, "Hey, Mom, it's me, Nola."

"I'm back here in the kitchen," she hollered back at me.

I made my way through the dining room and found Mother busily scrawling on some 3x5 cards spread out on the kitchen table. She was printing carefully and slowly as if it hurt her hand to write.

"What are you doing?" I asked.

"Oh, now Olive wants copies of some of my recipes and Nellie has asked for a few more. I don't know what's gotten into those two, but they're both baking up a storm. Maybe it's the change in the weather."

"Mother, I could always make copies for you at the office, if you would simply ask. Save you the trouble of all that writing. By the way, how's your arthritis?"

"I didn't want to bother you, Nola, with all the work you have to do. Besides, this gives a more personal touch, don't you think? And my arthritis is much better, thank you, now that I'm taking the same medication Myrtle takes." She put the pen down and flexed her fingers.

"Well, I wanted to stop by and see how you're doing. So far I haven't figured out where Myrtle is, but a missing person report should be filed soon. I'm sure she'll turn up," I said with more doubt than conviction.

"I sure hope so, Nola. Iris has been so worried about her, poor thing," Lillian remarked. "She's hoping she'll be back soon."

"Oh, really? She didn't seem that concerned when I talked to her a while ago."

"Well, maybe that's because I told her you were investigating Myrtle's disappearance."

"What? I'm not officially investigating anything, Mother. That's police business. I was looking into it for your sake, since you seemed so upset." My level of frustration was rising.

"Oh, I'm not upset anymore, now that I realized she must have gone to Dowd to pick up more of her arthritis medicine."

"Why? She doesn't see Doctor Barber and get her prescription filled at the local drug store?"

"Well, yes . . . and no. She does both. That way she can share some with me."

"Mother! That's not only illegal, it isn't safe. Why don't you see Doctor Barber yourself?"

"That silly old man. He's off his rocker, I say. He must be getting senile or else that German disease. I wouldn't go to him if he was the only doctor in town," Lillian huffed.

"German disease? You mean Alzheimer's? And he *is* the only doctor in town. Why do you say such things, Mother?"

"The other day Nellie took me with her to the market and we ran into Doctor Barber. He was in the liquor section about to pick up a bottle of brandy when we surprised him. He began talking gibberish about admiring the different colored bottles, sizes and shapes. All the while laughing like a maniac. Is that the kind of doctor you want me to be seeing?"

"Maybe he was embarrassed because you cornered him in a personal moment. Besides, what were you two doing in the liquor section?" I asked out of curiosity.

"We needed some rum so Nellie could make my rum cake recipe. Not so good without the rum, ya know."

"Mother, you know I routinely take you to the grocery store every Saturday. Why did you have to go with Nellie? Was there something else you needed that couldn't wait? I could always pick up a few items during the week, if need be."

"Actually, she needed me to buy the rum for her."

"You mean Nellie didn't have the money?"

"No, she didn't want anyone to see her buying it. She's funny like that. I personally don't care who sees me buying rum."

"I give up," I admitted. "Who am I to meddle in senior affairs? Speaking of affairs . . ." I hesitated to bring up what I saw on my way there, but forged right ahead, "I think Blanche and Officer Jeff are having one."

"One what?" Mother asked innocently.

"An affair. I saw them coming out of one of her listed properties on my way over here. Looked pretty chummy to me."

"Yeah, you're probably right. Myrtle suspected the same thing and told me she threatened to tell Jeff's wife if Blanche didn't cut it off. Blanche denied it, of course, but she wouldn't explain why she'd been spending so much time with him."

"Oh, really? So Myrtle found out and talked to Blanche about it? What about Charlie, does he know?"

"I'm not sure. But even if he did, he probably wouldn't do anything about it. He knows she'd never leave him because she's waiting to get her hands on Myrtle's fortune. And he likes keeping her around as a showpiece. She's one of those, you know, what do you call them . . . ?"

"Trophy wives?"

"Yeah, but for the life of me I've never understood your generation. I mean, your father would never have left me for a younger woman. It simply wasn't done back then. We stuck together through thick and thin, and that's the way it should be." She slammed her hand on the table and winced.

"I know Marty and I would have grown old together if he hadn't been killed, if that's any consolation."

"I know, Nola, and I didn't mean to imply that you wouldn't. Now, let me finish these recipes. Would you mind taking them to Nellie and Olive on your way back to the office?"

"Sure. No problem. But first I want to see that prescription bottle," I demanded.

"But I only have one pill left. That's why I figured Myrtle must be in Dowd. I told her I was running low," Lillian whined.

"I want to see it anyway, Mother," I repeated more forcefully.

"Oh, alright. It's on the window sill over the kitchen sink."

I picked up the bottle of capsules and read the prescription. Meclofenamate. I would have to look that up in the physicians' desk reference back at the office, but I was pretty sure it was nothing more than a non-narcotic pain reliever. I slipped the container into my pocket.

"Mother, I'd prefer you take an ibuprofen when your arthritis is bothering you. Those tablets weren't prescribed for you so I'm taking the bottle with me. No telling what that medication has been doing to your system. How long have you been taking this? And how often?"

Lillian was beginning to look scared. "Only for a couple weeks and only when I have pain. Why?"

"Because, and I repeat, they weren't prescribed for you. Look, if you don't like Doctor Barber, and you'd like to start seeing a doctor in Dowd, I'll drive you. Understood?"

Lillian put on her most convincing pouty face and said, "Fine, Nola. I guess my mind wasn't thinking clearly . . ."

"Exactly. Don't take any medications without me knowing about it. Agreed?"

"Agreed." She picked up the index cards. "Here!" she blustered as she handed me the recipes.

I took the cards and headed out the front door.

It just so happens that Nellie and Olive live only a few blocks apart. Nellie lived closest to mother's house, but I decided to go to Olive's first.

On my way over there, it occurred to me that I had never questioned Mother's instinct that Myrtle had gone to Dowd for her prescription. I mean, she'd been missing for days now. Didn't Mother find that odd? Or, did she know about Myrtle's secret lover? Something told me that I'd never get that piece of information out of her.

Olive was back home from the botanical society and sitting in a rickety wooden rocker on her front porch. An overweight orange cat was taking up her entire lap. She had removed her scarf, exposing a head of sparse red-dyed hair. It looked curlier than I remembered it before chemo, but since Olive owned the only hair salon in town, I guessed that would explain it.

She waved as I got out of my car, as if she was expecting me.

"Lillian called to tell me you were on your way," she said as I walked up to the house.

I climbed the steps and handed her the set of recipe cards. She kept on rocking and petting the orange cat, a beatific smile on her face. Baking smells emanated through the screen door. Something chocolate was my guess.

"Sit a spell, Nola. It's such a glorious day, don't you think?" She motioned with her free hand to a straight-backed chair.

"I really need to get to the office, Olive," I said, "and, yes, it is lovely weather we're having," I said as I started back down the steps, turning around at the bottom.

She hadn't seemed to hear me, and continued, "I remember days like this when Myrtle, Buddy, Florence, Ernie and I used to go down to the swimming hole. I was always the fifth wheel, as they say, because I didn't have a boyfriend. It was hard being around those lovebirds, but we had a lot of fun." She lifted up the sleeping cat and put it down next to the rocker, but the cat jumped right back up onto her lap.

She then picked up where she had left off. "It was a shock when Myrtle married Ernie. Of course, Florence was furious. Everyone had assumed Myrtle and Bud would get married when he got out of the service. But no, Ernie dumped Florence for Myrtle. I always thought he liked her better. I guess he saw his chance when Bud was sent overseas. Poor Florence. She never saw it coming. But I did. I could tell by the way Ernie looked at Myrtle. He never looked at Florence that way. She was so devastated. Probably why she never married, poor soul. I, myself, never cared much about men . . ."

I stood frozen in place. Olive seemed to be walking down memory lane all by herself. She was rambling and rocking faster as if she was unaware I was still standing there. The cat finally jumped down and scurried away.

"Florence was dating Ernie back in high school?" I said to get her attention.

She finally looked in my direction. "What, dear? Now, where did that cat go?" She stood up, looked around the porch and over the railing. "Georgia? Georgia Peach? Where are you?" she sung out, and then turned around and went inside.

"See you later, Olive," I hollered as the screen door slammed shut behind her.

9

Driving over to Nellie's, I tried to imagine Florence dating Ernie and I couldn't visualize it. Unlikely couple, in my opinion. Ernie was a nice looking man, as I recalled. He and Myrtle had made a handsome couple and always seemed happy, especially after Charlie was born. They doted on him and spoiled him rotten. Ivy, who came along much later, seemed to be ignored. But that was simply my teenaged impression. I never really knew her since she was behind me in school. Charlie and I were in the same class, and I couldn't stand him. So full of himself he was.

I was also puzzling over Olive's odd behavior. I didn't know her that well, but there had been a distinct change in her demeanor since I had seen her earlier at the botanical society. Maybe some kind of meds she's taking, I thought, even though there wasn't much doctors could do to ease the discomfort associated with chemotherapy. I'd been reading about medical marijuana being available in some of the larger cities, but Cider Crossing was so far behind the times it would be years before we caught up. Of course, word on the street was that marijuana might soon be legalized for recreational use, even though it would still be illegal at the federal level. Nevertheless, whatever Olive was taking, she was certainly feeling no pain.

Nellie wasn't home when I went to drop off the recipe cards, so I gave them to Junior and then headed over to the office.

The first thing that got my attention as I drove up was the shiny, new plate-glass window. Harold had obviously come and gone already, even though it was still morning.

I greeted Dora who was cleaning off the counter when I walked in. I could tell Cal was talking on the phone behind his partition. "Okay, officer. Thanks."

"Who was that?" I inquired as I approached his desk.

"Officer Frye," Cal answered.

"Oh . . . Jeff . . . and . . . ?"

"Nothing. No more body parts have turned up, well, at least no new ones. It seems the finger is not the one missing from the hand. It was a partial index finger. So, I guess that's an additional body part. No word from the lab. This story is going nowhere fast," Cal sighed.

"Well, we now have more time before the next edition goes to the printer. I'm sure they'll know something by then," I assured. Realizing I hadn't told him about Myrtle's disappearance, I added, "There *is* someone in this town that can't be accounted for and I'm hoping the body parts aren't hers."

Cal perked up. "Who?" he queried.

"Myrtle Maxwell."

"What do you mean 'can't be accounted for'?"

"Well, she's missing and nobody knows for sure where she could be or how long she's been gone. From what I've gathered, no one's seen her for almost a week now."

"Sheesh! Maybe we'll have a story after all. I can see the headline now: Myrtle Maxwell Meets Her Maker," Cal grinned.

"Calvin Smythe. That's not a bit funny," I admonished him, though I was amused by his rare attempt at levity.

"I'm sorry. I couldn't resist the alliteration," he apologized while scratching his short, graying hair.

"Well, I'm asking around and hope to get to the bottom of this soon. Meanwhile, we still need to leave space for the story . . . whoever it turns out to be."

"Yes, ma'am," Cal raised his hand in salute.

"Calvin, whatever's come over you?" I chided as I picked up the week's edition from the fresh stack on the front counter.

"Overworked and underpaid, I guess." And with that he turned back to his computer.

I quickly leafed through the day's paper. Nothing that exciting since we didn't run the body parts story.

Realizing Cal wouldn't be much help in finding Myrtle, I sat down at my desk to think while I transferred the recent photos from my camera to the computer.

By all accounts, Myrtle seemed to have been gone for days. It looked like she had left in a hurry. She was boiling eggs, so what time of day would that be? No help there. Were any lights left on? Darn, I couldn't remember. Charlie suspected something but he wasn't talking. Buddy, in Dowd, claimed he hadn't seen her in years, but I was almost certain he wasn't telling the truth. Blanche didn't seem overly concerned because she suspected her mother-in-law was visiting some mystery boyfriend. I suspected that her secret affair was with Buddy. Could it be someone else? Blanche was probably wishing she'd never return. For some reason, not a lot of townspeople were worried about Myrtle. I'd mentioned to Jeff that Myrtle appeared to be missing, and he should talk to Charlie, but had anyone reported her missing yet?

The photos were finished being transferred. I viewed them all, picked out the best ones, slugged them, moved them to the images file on the desktop and started to write cutlines for each when it occurred to me that I wouldn't know who the winners were until the next day. I'd end up taking more photos anyway, so I shelved the task. By then it was almost noon and Dora was getting ready to leave for the weekend.

This brought me back to the Myrtle enigma. I decided to call Jeff to see if a missing person report had been filed.

Jeff didn't answer his cell phone. Probably wasn't on duty or having another rendezvous with Blanche. *Shame on me*, I chastised myself. Alright, I'll have to go down to the police station, I resolved.

I gathered my stuff, told Cal where I was headed and was out the door in less than thirty seconds.

* * * *

"Now what?" I said out loud to the dashboard as I drove through town. I was hearing a sputtering sound coming from under the hood of my silver sport utility vehicle. I'd had it in the shop recently for a brake job and didn't want to spend any more money on repairs so soon. The sputtering stopped when I accelerated so I figured the problem was solved. But if it happened again . . . I'd worry about that later.

There was one patrol car plus the captain's vehicle parked in front of the station. I pulled into a visitor slot.

"Hi, Elsa Mae," I greeted the seasoned desk clerk. "Is Jeff, or rather, Officer Frye, on duty?"

"No, he doesn't come on until this evening. Can I help you, Nola?"

"Well, I need to find out if anyone ever filed a missing person report on Myrtle Maxwell."

"Came in yesterday," Elsa Mae answered quickly. "Took the call myself."

"What do you mean 'came in,' didn't Jeff talk to Charlie?"

"I don't know about that, but I had to fill out all the paperwork myself and get a copy to the sergeants for briefing."

"Who called it in, it wasn't Charlie?"

"I don't think so. Some man, though. Wouldn't give his name. Wanted to remain anonymous. I'm pretty sure it wasn't Charlie."

I was puzzled. "Don't you have caller ID on your office phone?"

"Heck, no," Elsa Mae replied. "It's only the regular line anyway, not for emergencies. They take those calls through the communications center in Dowd."

I knew that our local police service was contracted through the county, so our budget was limited.

"Is the non-emergency line listed in the local phone book?" I continued.

"Of course, under Cider Press Station, why?"

"Oh, nothing, I'm thinking out loud is all. So, what kind of information about the missing person did this guy provide?" I took out my notepad and prepared to take notes.

"The usual. Full name, date of birth, physical description, vehicle description, et cetera. He really didn't know a lot. Hung up before I finished with the questions."

"Did he say why he thought she was missing?"

"Yeah, something about not showing up for an appointment in Dowd." Elsa Mae turned to her desk and rifled through some papers. "Here it is, 'subject no show last Monday when expected around 1 p.m.' Reporting party said he hasn't been able to contact her by phone since then."

"Could I get a copy of that report, Elsa Mae? If she doesn't turn up by our deadline I'll run a short story and see if it helps us find her."

"Sure, Nola, hang on a sec." Elsa Mae headed to the copy machine and I put my notepad away.

The door to the back offices opened and Captain Peachtree stepped out. He was a tall, broad-shouldered and handsome man. He wore his uniform well, and his sandy blond crew cut made him look younger than he was. He was relatively new to his position, having moved here from the SoCal area just before I had returned home. I didn't know him that well, but had encountered him on several occasions.

He noticed me right away. "Nola. How're you doing? Is there anything I can do for you?"

"I'm fine. I just came by to see if a missing person report had been filed on Myrtle Maxwell yet. Elsa Mae is helping me, thanks."

"Yeah, I'm aware she's missing. I'm sure we'll find her. Well, it's good to see you, Nola. Glad you moved back here. Hey, would you like to grab some lunch with me? My treat to welcome you back," he offered.

Surprised by his gesture, I responded, "I've got to get back to work, Captain Peachtree. But thanks anyway." Still baffled, I added, "Maybe some other time?"

"Okay, I'm gonna hold you to it." And with that he headed out to his car.

I took the copy of the report that Elsa Mae handed me and headed out to *my* car as the captain was driving away.

Back in my car, I read over the report, taking note of Myrtle's vehicle description. It dawned on me that neither I nor Charlie had checked to see if Myrtle's car was in her garage. Charlie probably didn't because he assumed she drove out of town, and *I* didn't because I had been going along with Charlie's assumption. That was then, this was now.

I started the car, listened for that sound again, didn't hear anything and drove off in the direction of Myrtle's house.

I didn't encounter any "love birds" on the way there, even though I passed several houses with Maxwell Realty signs planted firmly on the lawn.

I parked in front of Myrtle's house and made my way down the driveway to the detached garage in the back.

The large cantilever garage door was padlocked. Was that a good sign? To make sure, I tried the side door. Locked also. There was a grimy window next to the door with a prickly pear cactus planted beneath. I cautiously leaned over the cactus to see inside but the window was too dirty. There were some gardening gloves lying on the ground nearby, so I picked one up and used it to wipe the window pane, and then peered inside again. No car. Phew! At least we know she wasn't kidnapped.

Charlie must be right after all. I mean, who knew his mother better than he did? If *he* wasn't worried, why should *I* be? Still, something didn't seem right. Yes, something to do with the anonymous caller who reported her missing.

I gave the hibiscus plants another big gulp of water and returned to my car.

10

"Darn!" I hollered as I slapped my hand on the dashboard. Like that was going to help. I was hearing that strange noise again upon starting up my car. I didn't have the time to take it into the shop, and they'd be closed for the weekend, so I resolved to drive it in on Monday. Of course, if it broke down before that I'd have to have it towed in, but at least I could manage to get around town on foot—somewhat.

Still wondering who called in the missing person report, I thought I might call Buddy again to see if I could get him to tell me more, and maybe admit to being the one. And I also thought that I should talk to Ivy and see if she knew about the "appointment." But that would have to wait. I needed to find Charlie first.

With the irritating noise continuing under the car's hood, I drove down Main Street to the insurance/real estate office. Charlie's car was parked out front, but not Blanche's. Trying not to speculate on where she might be, I went on into the office.

Charlie was working at his desk at the back of the room. There were no enclosed office spaces or partitions. A door on the side wall indicated a unisex bathroom. He looked up as I entered.

"Hi, Charlie," I said as nicely as I could. "I was over at the police station a few minutes ago and found out that an anonymous caller had reported your mom missing. Did Officer Frye talk to you yet?"

He slammed his pen down on the desk, "Who?"

"Jeff. Jeff Frye. You know, police officer, wears a uniform and a badge, carries a gun?"

"Very funny, Nola. Yeah, Jeff stopped by and I told him Mother wasn't really missing. So, what's all the fuss about?"

"Why do you say that? I mean, someone else obviously thinks she is."

"Look, I told you before that it's none of your business, so butt out, okay?"

"Well, aren't we a bit touchy? Yes, it is my business. I'm a reporter, remember? And reporters get suspicious when someone hasn't been seen or heard from in almost a week, with no explanation to boot."

"You want an explanation? Okay, I'll give you one. She's over in Dowd sleeping with her lover, what's-his-name," he said with venom. "I followed her over there once. They meet at a motel on the outskirts of town. At least she always visits Ivy and the kids when she's in town. Some kind of grandmother, huh? Sneaking around like some kind of common . . ."

I cut him off before he could say something he would regret. "Does she know that you know about this?" I asked. The fact that an elderly couple was meeting for sex didn't faze me for some reason.

"No. And don't you dare tell her either, Nola."

"Why are you so sure that's what is going on? Couldn't there be another explanation?" At the same time I was thinking, *what other explanation*?

"What else could it be? I'm not that naive, you know," he replied as he picked up his pen and then threw it back down on the desk.

"You said, 'what's-his-name.' Do you know this man?"

"No, but Blanche thinks his name is George."

"Uh huh," I uttered knowingly. "Has she been gone this long before?" I continued while translating George to Greg to Buddy.

"No, but I wasn't always keeping track. I'm a busy man, you know."

"Do you know for a fact that's where she is and who she's with?"

"No, but it fits. I'm through worrying about her, okay? I just hope I don't end up with a stepdad. I couldn't take that. No way!"

"Doesn't your mother deserve to be happy? I mean, she's been a widow now for ten years."

"She's too old for romantic notions. She should be spending her time with her kids and grandkids." He picked up a stack of papers and scattered them across the desk. A strand of gray hair had dislodged itself from his pate.

"Well, it appears your mom has found some kind of happiness, despite your wishes. Why does that make you so angry?"

He combed a hand back through his thinning hair, repositioning the loose strand. "Look, Nola, I told you before, this is *not* your concern. Now, I've got work to do. Good bye." He slid a document across his desk, picked up his pen, hunched over and began writing. The wisp of hair had dislodged itself once again.

Charlie was dismissing me, for the umpteenth time. I started for the door, and then turned back around. "What if she really *is* missing, Charlie? Shouldn't that be *your* concern?"

Charlie, scribbling away, ignored my rhetorical question, so I continued out the door.

11

Frustrated with Charlie's lack of alarm about his own mother, I told myself *to heck with it.* Besides, I needed to get some work done. I'd neglected to set up interviews with the awards nominees the day before, so that would be first on my agenda.

Even though I only worked part time, and made my own schedule, I still felt an obligation to put the newspaper first. Especially while my editor was off fly fishing in some remote area of Alaska; a guarantee he would be beyond cell phone coverage.

Might as well get started on the community awards profiles, I had decided.

Back at my desk, I opened the press kit and spread out the pieces. One pitch letter, unnecessary; executive director's business card wedged in the little slots on the inside pocket, also unnecessary; a copy of the article about last year's winners; a press release announcing this year's event; the mission statement of the chamber of commerce; and six brief biographies.

I pulled out the bios of the six nominees for Citizen of the Year. The other awards to be handed out were: Teacher of the Year, Volunteer of the Year and Business of the Year.

Joe Dana, retired railroad engineer, dedicated to youth sports activities. Margaret Sampson, retired teacher, chairperson of local scholarship fund. Betty Rayburn, organizer of the town's food and clothing closet. James Hackney, president of the historical society. Dr. Cecil Barber, general humanitarian. Myrtle Maxwell, organizer of the local animal rescue group.

Even if Myrtle was opting to skip the flower show, she certainly would show up for the community awards dinner, right?

Unable to reach Joe, Margaret, Betty or James by phone for interviews, I left them all messages. I even called Myrtle's house just in case she had returned. No answer, so I left her a message, too.

Finally, I reached Dr. Barber. He sounded a bit groggy, as if I'd awakened him from his afternoon nap, but he agreed to meet with me. We opted for one of the town's watering holes, Hernando's Hideaway. Original, I know.

I ran into Cal on my way out. He was fumbling through his camera equipment bag in the backseat of his car.

"Any more body parts show up?" I asked.

"No, and I don't have time for that anyway. We may have to forget about it. I've got to get started on next week's issue and I haven't even prepared the layout," he grumbled.

"You mean *we've* got to get the layout ready," I reminded him.

"Sorry, it's just that there's so much to do and I'm feeling a lot of pressure right now. Julius is counting on me . . . I mean, *us*." A look of chagrin passed over his face.

"Well, I'm on my way to interview Doctor Barber, and then I'll be back to help get some of the pages set up with ad placement. Figure out what else you want me to do, okay?"

I jumped into my SUV, cranked her up and listened for the strange noise as I made my way over to the Hideaway. The engine hummed like normal.

Cecil Barber was waiting for me at the bar, talking to Mort the bartender. Two other patrons were playing a dice game at the other end. Only one of the booths was occupied.

I motioned Cecil over to an empty booth that was toward the back. Grabbing his drink, he joined me. The gray suit he was wearing looked slept in and his gray hair looked out of order.

"How are you, Doctor Barber?" I asked politely as I slid onto the cracked, burgundy vinyl banquette. I removed my notebook, pencil and tape recorder from my bag and set them on the table. The doctor slid in across from me and set his drink on the table after taking a sip.

"Oh, I guess I'll live," he chuckled. "So, you want to know all about me, huh?"

"Just the highlights, but, of course, details of some of your good deeds."

"Just doin' my job, I say."

"Oh, yeah. According to the Hippocratic Oath, something about doing no harm?" I said to impress him with my limited knowledge.

"Actually, the exact words 'first do no harm' are not contained in the Latin version. Anyway, I prefer the Lasagna Oath myself."

I started laughing out loud immediately. "Yeah, right, the one that Italian doctors swear to? But you're not Italian, are you?" I continued laughing as Mort glanced over at me.

"No, I'm not. But I *am* serious. There is a modern version by that name which was written by Doctor Louis Lasagna in nineteen-sixty-four. I honestly don't remember the entire thing, but I do believe it to be more appropriate in today's society. He mentions the 'joy of healing.' I ascribe to it because Lasagna, who was also a professor and dean, removed the religious tone and prayer. He also says one must not 'play at God' either."

"Really? That's interesting," I commented.

"If you ask me, religion and medicine should not be intertwined. Unlike Christian Science, which is plainly an oxymoron in my opinion. I believe you should do what is best for the patient regardless of popular belief," he concluded. "There, I've made my point, so let's move on."

His statement had me puzzled, but I continued. "Okay." I switched on the recorder. "So, you went to medical school in Michigan?"

"Yes. University of Michigan, total emersion, hands-on training back in the early 60's. The clinical training I received helped me decide to become a general practitioner, a *rara avis* these days."

"*Rara avis*? Oh, yeah, rare bird," I translated. "So, how did you come to bring your practice to Cider Crossing?"

"Well, my wife was suffering from asthma and she needed to live in a drier climate. She was much better off here . . . that is until she was diagnosed with breast cancer. More of a death sentence back then than it is nowadays. Even with the primitive treatment of the times, she lasted a little over two years. I still miss her a whole bunch." Cecil stared down into his whiskey glass.

"I'm so sorry to hear that, Doctor," I empathized.

"Wish I could have helped her through the pain and suffering back then like I've been able to help others these days."

"Others? Like how? I know you've been shuttling patients back and forth to Dowd for their chemo treatments. Is that what you mean?"

"That, and the support sessions." He cleared his throat. "Sometimes you have to work around the system for the greater good, ya know?"

"You conduct support sessions for Olive, Archie and the others?"

"Yes, and anyone else who needs them. It's the right thing to do. I also pitch in at QuikMed when they need me."

"Quick . . . Med? Oh, right, the local clinic. So, how are these support sessions considered working around the system?"

"They just are. Now, turn that dang thing off," he said, indicating my recorder.

I hit the stop button. "Doctor?"

"Well, this town's so behind the times it doesn't provide that kind of service. Oh, yeah, you can go into Dowd for group therapy, but you get mixed in with a bunch of strangers and feel uncomfortable. What I do is much more personal, let's say." He slammed back the remainder of his drink and got up to order another.

I suspected the drink he was ordering wasn't his second one of the day, so I quickly went over my notes, deciding I had enough information for a short bio and would not need to engage in any further inebriated conversation. I *did* want to ask him about Mother's "borrowed" prescription, however, but I wasn't sure how to broach the subject.

Barber weaved his way back to the booth, fresh drink in hand, without spilling a drop. Amazing.

"By the way, did you know that Myrtle Maxwell is missing?" I had quickly decided to throw that question out there.

"Missing? What makes you say that? I just saw her the other day. Well, maybe a week ago or so. Come to think of it, she was supposed to call me when she got back, but she hasn't." He took a big swig of whiskey.

"Got back? From where?" I asked.

"Uh, I think she was going over to Dowd to visit Ivy."

"Well, apparently Ivy hasn't heard from her either. And Charlie is not being that helpful. Hopefully, she'll show up soon. I know the authorities are aware because an anonymous caller filed a missing person report this morning. I haven't been able to tell if they are following up on that yet, however."

"I'm sure it's just a miscommunication," assured Cecil as he downed what liquid was left in his glass and looked over at the bar.

"I wanted to ask you something," I said as I gathered up my stuff. "Why would you write two prescriptions for the same medication for Myrtle

Maxwell? She's given one of them to my mother for her arthritis."

"There must be some mistake. Besides, why wouldn't your mother come to me if she needed a prescription? I'd be more than happy to accommodate her."

I didn't want to get into that with him, so I simply agreed there must be some mistake and thanked him for the interview.

"Never mind," I said as I got up to leave.

12

By the time I arrived back at the office my stomach was reminding me that I was starving.

I stuck my head into the office doorway. "Cal, I'm going home to fix something to eat," I hollered. No response. "Cal?" I stepped further inside.

The muted sound of a one-sided conversation was coming from behind Cal's partition. I rounded the corner as Cal held up his index finger, indicating for me to wait a moment.

"Thanks, Officer Frye," Cal said before hanging up the phone. Looking up at me he relayed, "No news on the various body parts. These things take forever. Don't they know we have a paper to get out?" he ended on a whine.

"Cal, we have almost a week before we hit deadline. Besides, I thought you weren't going forward with that story until we had more info," I reminded him.

"I wasn't. But I'm trying to decide whether or not to leave room for it. Cripes! This is getting aggravating."

"Well, I'm going home for a while, but I promise to return."

"I'll be here alone all night at this rate," he mumbled as he turned back to his computer.

"No you won't, because I'll be here to help," I insisted before heading out to my car to drive the three blocks home. I parked on the driveway off the alley next to my house.

As I let myself in my side kitchen door, Bertie squawked at me from the front parlor and began to sing. When's the last time I fed and watered that pesky cockatoo? Or cleaned his cage, for that matter. Putting my purse down, I grabbed the bag of birdseed from the pantry on my way to check on the bird. As I passed by the phone I noticed the message light was blinking.

Returning to the kitchen I was accosted by Flossie, who was also begging to be fed. Taking care of that task also, I decided to toss something into the microwave for myself to eat.

As the frozen dinner was being zapped, I finally took a moment to check the phone message. It was Betty Rayburn, returning my call. I decided to clean the cat box first, and then call her.

I returned Betty's call and asked to meet with her at the flower show the next day. She told me she wouldn't be there because she had sprained her ankle and would be off her feet for a while. I told her if I finished covering the flower show early enough I would head out to her place that afternoon. Otherwise, I asked if Sunday would be alright, to which she replied that either would be fine since she wasn't going anywhere. She added that even though she wasn't entering any flowers in the show she would be sorry to miss the event.

I told her I would call her when I was on my way.

After I scarfed down my microwaved spaghetti, I headed back to the office.

"How's it coming along, Cal?" I greeted him as I came through the door.

"I could get a lot more done if the dang phone would stop ringing," he groused.

"Who's been calling? Any news from law enforcement?"

"Nah. All for you. Messages are on your desk. Betty Rayburn said she'd call you at home. Now, let me get back to work. Oh, and Page Three needs attention."

When I got to my desk, I scooped up the messages and saw that they were return calls from three of the community awards nominees. I called them back, one by one, and conducted the mini-bio interviews over the phone to save time. I should have done that with Betty, I thought, but the drive up to her place would be a nice change of scenery.

I cleaned up the layout of Page Three and asked Cal if there was anything else he needed me to do. He was playing his martyr role again when he insisted he had everything under control, so I might as well go home.

Not one to argue with him (much), I let myself out, locked the door behind me and drove back to the house.

Once again, my message light was blinking as I entered the parlor. It was getting late, and I hoped it wasn't Mother again. It wasn't. It was Greg. Or

Buddy, as he wished to be called. His message was cryptic, but he sounded urgent to talk to me. Great! Maybe a breakthrough. I picked up the receiver and sat down on the settee.

"Hi, Buddy, you wanted to talk to me again?" I said as nonchalantly as I could when he answered.

"Hey, Nola, thanks for getting back to me so soon," Greg responded. "I'm glad I kept your number in my caller ID. Yes, there's more I need to tell you."

"About your history?" I asked in an innocent tone of voice.

"No, about Myrtle," he confessed.

"Oh, I see, what about her?" Come on Greg, spit it out, I said to myself.

"I think she's missing. No, I'm *sure* she's missing." His voice had started to waver.

"What makes you say that?" Slow and steady, I coached myself.

"I wasn't totally honest with you yesterday when I said I hadn't seen her for years," he admitted. "I just saw her two weeks ago. She's been coming over to Dowd to see me for several years now. She also visits her daughter Ivy or picks up prescriptions when she's in town. Ivy knows about us. Anyway, she was supposed to be here Monday but never showed. We've been meeting at the El Rancho Motel here in town, usually on a Monday or Wednesday when my wife is at her dialysis appointment. I called her home several times, but got no answer. I didn't leave a message because . . . well, you know."

Now we were getting somewhere. "So, are you the anonymous caller who reported her missing?"

"Yes, that was me. I was hoping she'd show up on Wednesday instead, but when that never happened I decided I had to do something. I had to wait the required 48 hours, and it was killing me. I really care about her. I always have." He sounded as if he was about to cry.

"Buddy, I don't mean to pry, but it sounds like you and Myrtle have been having an affair."

He cleared his throat, hesitated, and then said, "Yes, we have. I couldn't help myself. I never stopped loving her, even though I married Greta and she was married to Ernie. Then Ernie died, and Greta's been ill for some time now. It just seemed like we were meant to be together again," he sniffled.

"And Myrtle was okay with you cheating on your wife?"

"Well she felt bad about it, but she understood that my role as husband had turned into more of a caregiver, if you know what I mean."

"So, it's kinda obvious that your wife had nothing to do with Myrtle's disappearance if she's that ill."

"She's very weak and in a wheelchair, so I would never suspect her at all. The doctors don't think she'll be around too much longer."

"I'm sorry to hear that, Buddy."

"Thank you, Nola. Are they trying to find her? Nobody will tell me anything. I even talked to Ivy, but she said she knows nothing either. She knew about us, but promised me that she had never told anyone."

"What about Charlie? Have you talked to him?"

"No. And I never want to. According to Myrtle, he's been trying to control her every move all these years since his dad died."

"Well, I have talked to him several times, and he's been keeping a tight lip about the whole thing. He alluded to being suspicious of his mother seeing someone, but I don't think he suspects it's you. I got the impression he wanted to put a stop to whatever was going on, however. He seems convinced that's why she's so-called missing, which also explains why he never filed a police report."

"Some doting son, eh? All he wants to do is to take over her empire. At least that's what I think. And I wouldn't trust his wife either, if you ask me." He cleared his throat again. "You don't think they had anything to do with her disappearance, do you?"

"I don't know what to think at this time," I sighed.

"Well, if you find out anything, anything at all, I want to be the first to know. After the police are informed, that is."

"Sure, Buddy. I'll be in touch. By the way, I'm not really writing an article about Cider Crossing High grads, I decided to use that as an excuse to talk to you. Find out if you knew anything about Myrtle's disappearance."

"How did you find out about me?"

"Myrtle's yearbook. Blanche pointed me in that direction."

"Oh. Well I'm glad you did. Once again, please let me know what's going on if you can. I'm getting more worried every day."

We hung up and I sat there pondering. Since her car was gone, it occurred to me that maybe she had been on her way to Dowd and ran off the road or something. Wouldn't the police have checked on any accident reports? Or checked with hospitals? I decided to call Jeff.

"Hey, Jeff, it's Nola. It's about Myrtle Maxwell. Several people I've talked to have suggested she was going to Dowd when she went missing. They offered a variety of reasons for thinking that. All I know is that her car isn't in her garage. Has anyone checked with the highway patrol or any hospitals?"

"Not sure, Nola. I think the case is being assigned to the detective squad in Dowd. I'll check on it and get back to you when I can, okay?" He sounded distracted and I could hear his radio squawking in the background.

"Thanks, Jeff," I ended the call.

13

Saturday morning I headed to the botanical society clubhouse to finish reporting on the fall flower show. This would be the first of their events for me since I had arrived back in town.

The historic house was filled with attendees and entrants as well as the late summer fragrances of a plethora of autumn blossoms. I spotted asters, chrysanthemums, zinnias and others I couldn't identify. Olive and Winnie were standing side-by-side near their entries. Florence was bustling about and Iris was guarding her lemony rose bush.

I snapped a few more pictures and then snagged Florence to find out when the winners would be announced.

"It's just a simple popular vote for first, second and third ribbons in each category. The guests receive a ballot when they pay the nominal attendance fee, so we won't be able to tally the votes until tomorrow," she explained.

Great. I would still be working on the story on Monday, I presumed.

"Oh, alright Florence. I'll check back with you," I conceded.

I wandered around admiring all the floral arrangements, and trying to decide whether I should head out to Betty's place to conduct her interview. As I approached Iris, she turned and headed toward the back of the room, appearing to avoid someone.

Blanche had arrived and was passing out her business cards to strangers from out of town. Most likely tourists just passing through. Why would they be interested in buying property here? Maybe looking to relocate? Anyway, I guess that's what business people like Blanche do. They never miss an opportunity to put themselves out there.

Nellie Semple was escorting my mother into the room when I turned around. That was nice of her. I would have brought mother myself, but I had to work.

"Hi, Mom. Hi, Nellie," I greeted them.

"It smells wonderful in here," Lillian said. "Did you enter any flowers, Nola?"

"No, Mom. I've got my hands full with work and the remodel. No time for gardening. Maybe next year," I answered, although I doubted that would happen.

"That's okay, Nola," Nellie interjected. "Iris wouldn't take kindly to more competition anyway," she laughed.

Just then, Iris appeared again out of nowhere. She didn't react to Nellie's comment, however.

"Don't you grow anything?" Iris asked of me. There was a slight shovelful of snide buried in the question.

"Not this year, Iris," I retorted with a smile.

I turned to Mother and Nellie and said, "Well, I'll let you two enjoy the show. I have to get back to the office, and then I may run out to Betty Rayburn's to interview her for the Citizen of the Year Award nomination bio. I was hoping to catch up with her here today, but she told me she sprained her ankle and wouldn't be able to attend. If I don't get a chance to interview her today, then I'll have to do it tomorrow. Anyway, I'll take you grocery shopping later, Mom, okay?"

"That's okay, Nola, I don't need anything this week," she replied without taking her eyes off the mums she was admiring. Iris was still standing there as if impatiently waiting for me to leave.

"Are you sure? Well, I'll call you later."

"Yes, dear," Lillian murmured.

I thought of talking to Winnie and Olive again about Myrtle's whereabouts, but when I looked toward their displays I saw that they weren't standing nearby them any longer. That's when I glanced out the front window and saw them getting into Winnie's green SUV and driving off

It was strange that they didn't stay for the entire time. Perhaps they were running off to grab some lunch and would return. I dismissed their peculiar behavior, said my good-byes to whoever would listen and made my way out to my own car.

After I checked in at the office and completed a few tasks, I informed Cal that I had decided I had better drive out to Betty's and get that interview over with. Being hers was the last interview of the slate of nominees, except for Myrtle's, I could finally start writing them up.

His fingers were flying across the keyboard. No eye contact. No response.

"Cal?" I repeated, and received a grunt in return.

As I walked out to my car, I realized he hadn't heard a word I said.

14

Pete Seeger (not the folksinger) was the man who founded Cider Crossing in the mid-1920's. He had never intentionally set out to do so, but by some stroke of fate it simply came to be.

After serving his brief stint in the army during the Great War he had moved out to Hollywood to try his luck in the fledgling movie industry. All he had been able to achieve was a few parts as an extra in some silent films. He had taken on a few manual labor jobs also, just to make ends meet. Even though "talkies" were about to take off, Pete had become disillusioned with the glitz and glamour and had ditched his dreams of becoming a movie star.

Little did anyone know at the time that the Dust Bowl era was on its way, and a lot of those poor souls in the middle of the country would soon be migrating to California. Pete was about to be spared from all that suffering and grief.

Pete had been making his way across a desolate section of Southern California in his 1920 Ford pickup truck. The dirt road he was on was wending its way toward the National Old Trails Road which would soon become part of Route 66. He had stowed all his belongings in the bed of his truck and was headed back to his family's farm in Kansas, having become disappointed with his life Out West.

He had almost reached a one-lane bridge that crossed a wide creek when his truck conked out. It was obvious to him right away, from seeing the plume of steam shooting out from under the hood, that the radiator was overheated. Climbing out of the truck, he grabbed his brand new canvas water bag which hung from his radiator cap. It was a new Hirsch-Weis product with the picture of a red apple on the front and the silhouette of a leaping stag above. (Hirsch-Weis later became White Stag, which is the English translation from German of the two names.)

He then lifted the hood and, using a rag, he unscrewed the radiator cap. Since the water bag was only half full, Pete decided to let the radiator cool down while he went to fill up the bag down by the creek and rest for a spell. He descended the short bank of the creek next to the bridge and immersed the bag in the semi-cool water to soak for a while in the slow-moving current.

Sitting on a small boulder at the creek's edge, he was keeping an eye on the bag in case it tried to float away when he spotted a bright glint just under the surface. Reaching down to feel for what it was, he couldn't believe his eyes when he picked up a rather large gold nugget.

He sat there holding the nugget in his hand and wondering, in disbelief, if it could be real. He knew real gold would be heavy, and this nugget was. He also knew if he bit down on it, his teeth would leave an impression if it was the genuine article. So, he bit down on it. Sure enough, he left bite marks, so he put his precious find in his pocket.

Hoping there would be more gold to discover, Pete picked up the canvas bag, filled it with water, and then scrambled back up the bank and cooled the radiator. Then, searching the bed of his truck for something to pan gold with, he uncovered a cast-iron skillet which had been packed away. Shoving aside his heavy red gas cans, he grabbed the frying pan. This will have to do, he thought as he rushed back down to the creek bed.

All in all, Pete was able to retrieve eight gold nuggets of various sizes before he became worn out. Several vehicles had crossed the bridge during that time, causing him to suspend his activities for a bit. He had greeted them with a wave of his hand as they drove on, or shook his head if they hollered their offer of help. He couldn't wait to head back the way he had come and cash in his treasures. It would be a long trek, but it would be worth it.

Before exchanging his nuggets for gold certificates and applying to homestead 160 acres near where he found the gold, Pete had had an epiphany moment. He decided he would return to the gold discovery site and establish an apple orchard. He would grow apples and make cider to offer to passing motorists and would also sell his apples back in town. The brilliant idea had sprung from the apple logo on his Hirsch-Weis canvas water bag. It had been a sign, Pete reckoned, a very good sign. And Pete believed in signs.

So, he planted his orchard and laid out a temporary irrigation system by tapping into the nearby creek. He had staggered his four, forty-acre parcels along the creek below the bridge to allow the creek to run through his property, but he hired a dowser to pinpoint a location for a well.

He started building a rustic cabin for himself and then started work on the cider stand. It took several years for apples to appear, but by then Pete was ready for business. He had already purchased his cider press and began to set to work.

Later on, he would start a wooden crate-building factory. He, himself, would need crates to ship his apples, and he could also sell crates to other orchard farmers.

At first, business was slow, but soon the traffic began to pick up as more families were heading Out West. He had even taken the time, while back in town, to telegraph some family members in Kansas about his venture. Several relatives made the trek out to help him, and a few stayed on.

Once the crate factory was up and running and Pete had hired several people to work there as well as in the orchard, things started to snowball. Workers had to have homes to live in and businesses began to arrive to supply goods and services to the people. A one-room school house was built to serve the children of the growing resident population followed by facilities for law enforcement and fire protection to serve everyone. Pete was then able to build himself a nice one-story farmhouse by ordering a self-build kit from one of the mail-order companies that were cropping up at the time.

Before Pete knew it, he had established an unofficial town and had ceded all but 40 acres of his homestead to the town before he passed away.

Little by little, people had been moving in and it soon became necessary for the town to declare its name so it could establish its own post office. Cider Crossing was agreed upon almost unanimously at a town meeting, and Cider Crossing it still is today, with the addition of quite a few more square miles of land acquired over the years.

15

Cider Crossing's early history and its unique reason for continuing to survive were trickling through my mind as I drove along Oak Creek out toward Betty Rayburn's farmhouse—the one that Pete Seeger had built for himself after his success.

A rumor that had been passed down for several generations was that Pete had been fermenting hard cider on the sly during prohibition. He obviously would have had all the equipment to do so, since his primary legitimate business was producing regular apple cider. I began to wonder where he kept his secret operation. Maybe near Betty's house? It was just a thought.

It was another pleasant early fall day. Warm, not hot. Light breeze, no wind. I had called Betty to let her know I would be there that afternoon after all.

I hadn't ventured out this way in ages because there was hardly anything left standing to see. I did pass an outbuilding off to the side that stood next to a dilapidated cottage. The outbuilding appeared to be maintained, but the house didn't.

As I flew on past, I spied the rear end of a pick-up truck which was parked behind the building. Apparently, the structure was still being used in some way. I wasn't sure who owned the property, however.

Passing several apple orchards along the way, some active, some dormant, made me wonder why people stayed in this area. Some were descendants of the early pioneers and had never left, but some had left, only to return later on.

What was it about Cider Crossing? The temperate climate? The quiet, simple way of life? Or the somewhat lower cost of living? The crate factory was still going strong, but that was about it.

The town's magnetism was definitely a curiosity to me. Of course, I, myself, had returned to Cider Crossing. But, my main reason was to live closer to my mom. Besides, my life in Northern California had been disrupted when my husband was killed, so I had the latitude to live wherever I chose.

Both of my kids lived out on the West Coast and had their own lives. And I was not the kind of mom who wanted to intrude on them by moving in next door. At least I had driven down the coast on my move to Cider Crossing and had been able to visit with them both and their respective significant others. Neither offspring seemed eager to jump on the marriage wagon, but they appeared happy just the way they were.

They both promised to come visit me when they had some time off, and it only took six or seven hours to drive the distance. Flying was not an option since the nearest major airport was at least half-way there.

The mere thought of air travel made me wish I'd taken flying lessons when I was younger. I'd always had a fascination with Amelia Earhart, which is why I named my daughter after her. There was a tiny, private airport a short distance south of town. Maybe I should check it out sometime. I made a mental note to do so.

Okay, snap out of it and get back to business, I scolded myself.

I started running through a few questions to ask Betty when a glint up ahead on the right caught my eye.

There appeared to be a car parked down by the creek. As I got closer to the spot, I caught the sight of two women in modest bathing suits wading along the shore. They were holding hands and stepping carefully across the rocks.

I slowed down a bit, but couldn't make out their faces. Plus, the trees and bushes kept blocking my view. That's when I recognized the scarf on one woman's head. It was Olive and Winnie, confirmed by the make and model of the car—it was Winnie's SUV.

I had just put two and two together when I saw the two of them embrace and kiss. Not a peck, but a long, amorous smooch. Oh, my, I never would have guessed. I mean, Winnie was a married woman, but I guess that didn't matter. Come to think of it, I hardly ever saw her in the company of her husband. He was a traveling salesman, leaving her on her own for days at a time.

So, how long had this been going on? None of my business, I decided as I motored on to Betty's.

Hopefully, they didn't notice me—at least I didn't *think* they spotted *me* spotting *them*.

* * * *

The interview with Betty went well. Talking to her in depth had made me realize she was a genuinely caring person deserving to be acknowledged for her selfless contribution to our community. She even served tea and scones while I was there, despite the fact that I could tell her ankle was still bothering her.

Her work in establishing the Pots and Pants food and clothing facility for the needy was to be commended. I secretly hoped she won the Citizen of the Year award.

I thought of asking Betty if she had picked up any gossip about Winnie and Olive, but decided that wouldn't be very professional of me. Even though a reporter's job is to ferret out information, there was no story to follow, just a curiosity. So I kept my mouth shut.

I was on my way back to town when my car started making that odd sound again. I was risking getting stuck out there in the country if what I was hearing was the precursor to a major breakdown.

I held my breath and kept driving, passing the section of the creek where I had witnessed who-knows-what. The ladies were long gone, thank goodness. Of course, they could have come to my rescue, if need be.

Soon the noise ceased like before. One more day of uncertainty, and then I could drive it in to Mac's and have it looked at. I continued on into town.

I arrived home without incident, fed both the pets, and then called my mother like I said I would.

She still insisted that she had plenty of provisions to last for a while. In fact, she said she was cooking dinner for Florence and invited me over for spaghetti. I took her up on the offer. Real *homemade* spaghetti this time.

As I was getting ready to leavc for mother's house, the phone rang. It was Jeff informing me that the detectives had been doing their due diligence and had determined that Myrtle had not been in an automobile accident. He added that they were still investigating, and would be canvassing both Cider Crossing and Dowd for any clues.

I thanked him for keeping me informed and resigned myself to letting law enforcement do its job.

16

I arrived at my childhood home just as Florence was pulling up in her dusty old Honda. The car suited her to a T since it looked as frumpy as she always did.

"Hi, Florence, Mother said you were coming to dinner," I greeted her as she was extricating herself from her vehicle. "She invited me, too."

"Yea, spaghetti, my favorite," she said when she finally got herself upright and straightened her plain brown skirt while holding onto a shopping bag.

"Let's go on inside." I held the screen door open for her to enter first, and she clomped inside in her brown orthopedic shoes.

"I brought the garlic bread, Lillian," Florence hollered toward the kitchen area.

"Oh, good," Lillian hollered back. "The sauce is still simmering, but I haven't put the pasta in to boil yet." She appeared in the doorway and retrieved the proffered bread from Florence.

"Do you need any help, Mom?" I asked.

"No, no. Make yourselves comfortable in the living room and I'll bring out the wine. Glasses are in the china cabinet, dear. But, of course, you know that,

Nola," she sang out as she scurried back into the kitchen.

I retrieved the wine glasses and set them on the coffee table.

"Have you determined who the flower show winners are yet?" I couldn't help asking, ever the reporter I was these days.

"No. I was too tired after all the activity today to run a tally. The ballots are locked in a desk drawer, so I'll get to them in the morning. Of course, someone will have to be a witness. Someone who was not entered in the contest, that is. Since you're reporting the story, it can't be you, Nola. Maybe I'll get one of the boys to help me. Like Archie or Harold," she smiled.

Lillian finally appeared with the bottle of red wine. Uncorked already, no less. I poured half a glass for each of us and we toasted to the town of Cider Crossing for some reason. Then Mother rushed back to the kitchen to see if the *unwatched* pot was boiling yet.

"So, Olive was reminiscing yesterday about the good times you all had when you were young adults. She revealed that you and Ernie were dating back then." I knew I was taunting her, but I couldn't help myself once again. "I'd never heard that one before, even though Mom has told me lots of stories about her school days."

"That's old news by now. Anyway, what difference does it make? Myrtle stole him from me, that's all there is to it. I guess she couldn't wait for Buddy to get back from the war and she had to be with someone. Poor Buddy, he was devastated when she broke it off with him," she sighed. "Sent him a

Dear John letter, of all things. I never did like Myrtle. Always acted like she was better than everyone else." She picked up her wine glass and took a swig.

"You're a retired nurse, is that right?" I inquired for no reason.

"That's right. I was a nurse for over forty years. Why do you ask?"

"Oh, no reason. Have you heard anything about Myrtle's whereabouts? Apparently, she's been missing for quite a few days."

"So what? Good riddance is what I say. Maybe she's sprawled out dead in the desert. And the coyotes are snacking on her. Ha! A coyote snack!"

"That's a horrible thing to say, Florence! You must really hate her to wish her such a fate. Why else would you say such a thing?" Her attitude was so appalling it made me start to suspect her of foul play due to her being cuckolded.

"You don't remember what happened to Rosie Vasquez, do you?" Florence retorted. "Nah, you were too little back then to have been told the story. Anyway, she was a teenager who went missing over forty years ago. She was last seen buying a quart of milk at the mom and pop grocery store we used to have here. Her skeletal remains were discovered out in the desert over ten years later. They never could determine the cause of death, and they never caught the guy who did it either. Probably some transient passing through town is my guess."

"That's awful." I paused to collect my thoughts. "Florence, are you sure you don't know something about Myrtle's disappearance? Anything at all?"

"Of course not," she bristled. "What are you accusing me of, Nola?" She then stood up so abruptly she almost toppled the coffee table. Hands on hips.

"Whoa! I'm not accusing you of anything. I'm just trying to gather information, that's all," I rejoined to her overly defensive posture.

"Well, maybe you should talk to Winnie or Olive. They've got a secret," she snickered. "And Myrtle found out about it. I think they were afraid she might tell Winnie's husband. Some people will do anything to shut someone up." She sat back down.

I ignored her last statement. "What secret?" I asked, but I thought I may already know.

"That's for them to tell, not me," she huffed. Then, never one to follow proper etiquette, she added, "Now, when will dinner be ready? I'm starving!"

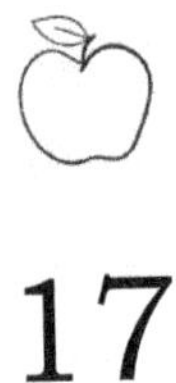

17

Sunday was usually a do-nothing day for me. I don't attend church, but Mother does. Her church is actually within walking distance of her house, but it's hard for her to get there when her arthritis flares up. One of the church ladies usually picks her up and drives her, so I have the day all to myself to do whatever I want. I can stay in my pajamas all day if I choose to do so. Unless I have to work, of course.

Since I still had to write up the mini-bios on all the nominees for Citizen of the Year, I thought I'd better do so. I had my notes from Betty's interview in my tote bag, but I had left the other ones at the office. I took a quick shower, threw on some casual clothes, gulped down a cup of coffee, and then grabbed my tote bag and headed over there on foot again.

Cal was typing away when I unlocked the door and entered. He looked like he hadn't slept in days.

"How is everything, Cal?" I tried to sound pleasant so as not to ruffle his feathers.

"What are we going to do about the body parts story? If we don't get more details soon I'm going to have to reassign the space I left open. Of course, we could run a short piece about the discoveries in hopes that someone may come forward with more information," he sighed. "I don't know, Nola. Can't you find out if there are any new developments by talking to Officer What's-His-Name?"

"Frye, Jeff Frye. I *did* talk to him, but it was more about Myrtle's disappearance. He said the detectives are working on it, and they don't think she was in a car accident. I hope and pray the two stories are not connected."

"The fact that Myrtle is missing is not a story. At least not yet," he declared.

"Don't say that, Cal. Okay, I'll check on the gruesome body parts and get back to you. Meanwhile, I've come to retrieve my notes for the upcoming awards dinner. You've left room for that article, right?"

"Front page, below the fold. Now let me get back to work."

"Yes, sir," I responded as I stuffed my notes into my bag. "Sheesh!" I added as I left.

I was strolling along the sidewalk heading back home when Jeff pulled up to the curb in his patrol car. He rolled down the passenger side window and greeted me.

"Hey, Nola. Hop in and I'll give you a ride," he offered.

"Hey, Jeff. Ya know, I've been wanting to go on a ride-along for some time now. How about right now?"

"We'll have to check you in back at the station, but sure. Do you have your ID on you?"

"Like they don't know who I am, huh?"

"Just police protocol, that's all," he explained.

"Am I even dressed appropriately?" I was wearing jeans, a plain light green T-shirt and tennis shoes.

"You wearing lace-up shoes?" Jeff asked because he couldn't see my feet.

"Yeah, why?"

"In case you have to run," he responded.

"Well, then I'm good to go. But I left my purse back at the house. Can we swing by there first?"

"Sure. Hop in."

* * * *

After we vetted me back at the station, and I signed some forms, we headed back out on Jeff's patrol route. His computer was mounted between us and his radio began sporadically crackling unintelligible transmissions. At least to me they were hard to comprehend. Jeff radioed back a few times, speaking the same lingo.

Marty would have understood the copspeak, but he had ceased his telepathic communications with me. I guess, after I moved back home, he became satisfied that I would be alright without him, so he had faded into the background. But I always knew he was there if I needed him. To get my mind off of Marty, I was hoping something exciting would happen. But, as the Monkees once sang, it was a Pleasant Valley Sunday.

When the radio quieted down, I asked, "Any new developments on the body parts?"

"I haven't heard anything yet. Maybe you should talk to Captain Peachtree."

"Oh, okay." More radio static.

During another lull, I remembered about the day I saw Jeff and Blanche having some sort of rendezvous. So, I decided to broach the subject. Carefully.

"Have you seen Blanche lately?" I asked as nonchalantly as I could.

"Who? Oh, you mean the realtor," Jeff answered while never taking his eyes off the road.

"Yeah. Charlie Maxwell's wife. I know you talked to Charlie about his mom, so you must have talked to Blanche also since she is Myrtle's daughter-in-law. In fact, now that I think about it, I thought I saw the two of you outside one of her listings the other day."

"I talked to her briefly, but it was at the . . ." he was interrupted by the radio. He garbled a response full of letters and numbers and we took off with lights and siren.

"Whoa! What's the call?" I shouted as I grappled for something to hold onto.

18

"Auto accident. Someone got run off the road and down an embankment, apparently."

Jeff was racing toward the creek side of town. His driving skills were impressive. As scary as the wild ride was, the precision with which he handled the vehicle made me confident we would arrive at the scene in one piece.

As we approached, I could see that the paramedics had beaten us there and were making their way down the bank toward the creek. A fire engine had also arrived, just in case the car caught on fire, I assumed.

Jimmy had climbed up the bank and was already surveying the area. He seemed to be looking for skid marks or the presence of tire treads along the roadway.

Jeff quickly radioed something which was totally incoherent to me, grabbed a camera, and then we both got out of the patrol car at the same time.

He immediately took off toward the center of activity. I held back, still somewhat in shock. I could only see the rear end of a silver vehicle that was pointing nose down.

As I got closer to the edge I could tell that the front end of the car was partially submerged in the creek water. I didn't recognize the car, although it looked very similar to mine. I could barely see some damage on the left rear. The driver hadn't been removed yet, so I wasn't sure who the accident victim was either. I prayed the person was unharmed and still alive.

I walked over toward Jimmy to see if he knew who was driving the car.

"Doctor Barber," he replied when I asked.

"Oh my god! What happened?"

"Hard to tell yet, but the doctor *was* able to call 9-1-1. Said someone ran him off the road. Of course, with his history of public intoxication, maybe he ran *himself* off the road." Jimmy didn't seem that concerned, but I was glad to hear Dr. Barber was still alive.

"Aren't you finding any evidence to corroborate his story?" As soon as those words left my mouth, I knew I had immediately launched into my reporter mode.

"Maybe, maybe not. Lots of tire marks, no skid marks, but there are fresh marks indicating someone may have taken off in a hurry and made a U-turn heading back into town. Hard to pinpoint the tread pattern though. From the looks of the damage, it's possible the doctor's car may have been bumped similar to a PIT maneuver used by law enforcement, and when he overcorrected he ended up going over the side. We'll have to determine if the damage is fresh or not, and also have forensics check for paint transfer."

"Pit maneuver? Is that cop lingo?"

"Yeah, I guess. P-I-T. It stands for Pursuit Intervention Technique among other things. It's a way of disabling a vehicle being chased by law enforcement."

"I may have heard my late husband use that acronym, come to think of it. Anyway, thank God he's okay. Or at least he's still alive, right?" I subconsciously crossed my fingers.

"EMS will take good care of him," Jimmy assured me.

I made my way back to the patrol car. I didn't want to get in the way of the emergency responders. Plus, I hadn't brought my tote bag along, so I didn't even have my camera to take pictures or my notepad to take down pertinent information. Drat! Some reporter I was turning out to be. I *did* have my cell phone in my purse, however, so I called the office to see if Cal wanted to cover this story.

Cal reluctantly agreed to drive over as soon as I was able to direct him to the location. "You know, the road along the creek heading north out to Betty Rayburn's place," was all I was able to provide.

"I know the way. I'll be right there," Cal replied crankily.

It occurred to me that this was approximately the same place I had spied Winnie and Olive having their romantic rendezvous the day before. A weird coincidence, but inconsequential, I decided. Or, at least it seemed so.

I watched as the paramedics carted Dr. Barber up the embankment on a stretcher and headed toward their emergency vehicle. He appeared to have a neck brace in place. They loaded him inside, and then all four climbed aboard, two in front, two in back, and they took off. The firemen were still inspecting the vehicle.

Jeff trudged up the hill also and came toward me. "I called for a tow truck to haul his car out of here," he said.

"Cal should be here any minute to take pictures," I informed him.

"I took a few myself. Not a big story, if you ask me," he declared. "He claims someone ran him off the road, and there is some slight damage to his left rear bumper, but I'm not so sure that's what happened here. He may have been drinking, so he'll have to be checked out at the hospital for that."

"Jimmy thinks the same thing. Are they taking him all the way over to Dowd?" I asked.

"For sure. They don't want to take any chances if he has any internal injuries. QuikMed isn't equipped to run all the tests needed, they said. I'll have to notify law enforcement over there to witness a blood draw, if necessary."

"This sure is strange," I commented. "I wonder where Doctor Barber was headed? Not much out this way. A few houses near the active orchards, but that's about it."

"Said he was on his way out to Betty Rayburn's to look at her sprained ankle. Can you contact Betty to let her know he won't be showing up after all? I've got to deal with the tow truck operation." He glanced over my shoulder toward the road. "And here they are."

I turned around to see Don's Towing Service arriving with Cal right behind.

"Sure thing. I'll call Betty and I'll get a ride back into to town with Cal since you'll probably be tied up for a while."

Jeff was already heading on over to greet the tow truck driver. "Thanks, Nola," he hollered over his shoulder.

Dang. I never did get an answer out of him about Blanche. I figured I'd have to talk to her instead.

19

Cal snapped a few photos of Dr. Barber's upended vehicle and then we returned to town in his car. We discussed the incident on the way back and we both decided on a captioned photo only. No story. Cal wasn't sure what page it would end up on yet.

Back at the office, I called Betty to tell her what had happened to Dr. Barber. She said that she was unaware he was on his way out to make a house call, and that she was sorry to hear about the accident. I asked her if there was anything I could do for her. She declined the offer for now, but said she'd let me know.

After we hung up, I then told Cal I'd be working on my bios at home since I'd left my tote bag there.

Once again, I took off on foot toward my house. But when Blanche drove by in the direction of her office, I decided to turn around and go talk to her again.

Speed-walking my way down the Main Street sidewalk, I made it to the front of the building she shared with Charlie just as she was getting out of her fancy vehicle. She grabbed her briefcase from the back seat.

As I walked around her front bumper, I noted that the bright red Cadillac Escalade appeared to be in pristine condition, so I ruled her out as Dr. Barber's road warrior right away.

"Hey, Blanche," I greeted her. "You won't believe what just happened a while ago. Doctor Barber was run off the road that runs along Oak Creek. His car ended up face down in the water."

"Oh, my gosh! Was he hurt?"

"Not sure yet. The ambulance is taking him to Dowd to be checked out."

"How did you hear about this?" Blanche wondered aloud.

"I was on a ride-along with Jeff when he got the call."

Blanche was flipping through her key ring with one hand, searching for the office key. "Come on in, I want to hear more."

She unlocked the door and we entered a darkened space before she flipped on the lights.

"No Charlie?" I asked.

"Not today. I work weekends, he doesn't," she complained. "Have a seat," she gestured toward one of the two guest chairs in front of her desk, and then plopped herself down behind it.

I sat myself down in the closest chair and placed my purse in the other one.

"So, there's not much else to tell," I picked up the conversation. "Why on earth would someone want to harm Doctor Barber? I mean, he's one of the good guys, right?"

"Well, not everyone thinks so. My mother-in-law for one." She started removing papers from her briefcase and placing them on her desktop.

"What? Why? Mother told me Myrtle gets her arthritis medication prescription from him. That should be a reason to approve of him, right?"

"Getting her prescription filled is necessary. What she doesn't like is that he tried to get her to join the MJ Club. Myrtle's adamantly against such a thing."

"The MJ Club? You mean as in Mary Jane, uh . . . marijuana?"

"Yeah. You didn't know about that? You being a reporter and all? Of course, Doctor Barber still thinks it's a secret. But half the town knows about it. So far, only those residents who are on chemo are involved, but he's trying to recruit others. Which is why it's not such a secret anymore."

"But medical marijuana is legal now, at least in some states, including ours. And recreational use may be coming soon. Although it's still considered illegal by federal standards, which is cause for debate. So what's the big deal? I know we don't have a dispensary here in town yet. But it shouldn't be long. Unless, of course, the town votes against it. Which it might. Meanwhile, those people who've been approved for an ID card can go to Dowd for their weed," I concluded my lecture.

"None of them have applied for cards, as far as I know. They would rather grow their own and stand united with Doctor Barber. Myrtle was totally against that, of course, and she threatened to turn him in. All of them, actually."

I started to think back to my encounters with Archie, Nellie, Harold and Olive. They all seemed to be doing extremely well, considering. And Olive and Nellie had been baking a lot lately. Probably weed brownies or cookies, I laughed internally. I should have figured this out sooner, I suddenly realized.

"And now Myrtle is missing, and Doctor Barber gets run off the road? None of this makes any sense," I admitted to Blanche.

"None of them took too kindly to her threatening to expose their little club. So, maybe one of them had something to do with Myrtle's disappearance. Just sayin'." She moved more papers around.

I should talk to each one of them separately, I thought. Maybe one of them would come clean with me.

The phone on Blanche's desk rang. She picked up the receiver and answered professionally, "Maxwell Properties."

I caught her eye, held up my finger and pointed toward the door. Slinging my purse over my shoulder, I moved toward the entrance and back outside. Daylight had not yet begun to fade.

I carried my plate of "food for thought" with me as I walked on home.

20

It occurred to me that I never got around to asking Blanche about my seeing her and Jeff together that day. Drat! But she had handed me a whole new bucket of information instead, so I couldn't complain. The marijuana club. I needed to talk to at least one of the members. But which one first, and how would I approach the subject? I wondered if my mother knew anything about it. Maybe I should talk to her first, and then go from there, I decided.

"Hi, Mom, how was church?" I inquired when she answered the phone.

"It was nice. I wish you would attend with me once in a while," she admonished. "Reverend Collins keeps asking about you."

"Maybe the next special occasion, okay? Meanwhile, I've had quite a day, so I thought I'd come over there and tell you all about it. Are you busy? Have you taken your cat nap yet?"

"I was just about to lie down. How about a couple of hours from now? I can put together an early dinner, if you'd like."

"Or, we can go to that new restaurant that just opened in the south part of town. We can decide later. I'll see you in a while."

I decided to spend part of the next two hours working on my bios. There were six of them to write, but I hadn't been able to interview one of them—and that was Myrtle. I typed up the other five, leaving hers for last. I could probably talk to the people at the animal rescue facility in her absence, but I could also talk to Charlie again.

I knew enough about Myrtle to put together her bio on my own, but having an excuse to gather more information about her disappearance seemed like a good idea. Problem was, unless I showed up at his house unannounced, I wouldn't know where else he could be on a Sunday. Maybe back at Myrtle's house checking up on the cat and such? I was pretty sure he was not a church goer, and I didn't want to have to ask Blanche if she knew what he was up to on his day off, so I might as well head to the outskirts of town where their custom-built house was located. I'd swing by Myrtle's first, just in case Charlie might be there, and then head to the south of town if he wasn't.

As I drove past Iris and Bert's house, I recognized Bert's late model Chevy Silverado pickup sitting in the driveway. Knowing Bertrand Pettis was no longer with us, I assumed Iris must have been driving it instead of her older Subaru.

Although Bertrand may have been named after Bertrand Russell, the multi-faceted political and social activist, he turned out to be the total opposite. From what I could recall, he was a self-centered, money grubbing bigot, who always had to have his way. He probably wouldn't cotton to Iris driving his blood-red pickup either. I'm sure he thought his color choice was perfectly appropriate for a butcher's vehicle. Maybe Iris was getting ready to sell it, I presumed.

Once again on Birch Street, I caught a quick glimpse of Blanche entering the same property as before, only this time there was no Jeff in sight. Maybe I had jumped to a conclusion about them, but I still wanted to know the real story. Curiosity doesn't *always* kill the cat, right?

Moving on toward Myrtle's house, I cruised up and down her street until I was sure no one was there. No Charlie.

Back out on Main Street, I headed south. A few miles later, I entered Charlie's somewhat ritzy neighborhood which had been dubbed Green Acres. The "acres" part I understood, being each individual structure, some manufactured, and some framed, stood on its own one-acre plot. The "green" part was a misnomer, however. Most of the grounds surrounding each home appeared to be either dirt or xeriscaped with rocks. Only a few green lawns could be seen throughout, including the lush 9-hole golf course I had passed on the way in.

It took me a while, wending my way through the community, to locate Charlie's house. Mother and I had been out here once before, attending a birthday party for Myrtle, but I had forgotten which house it was. I had almost passed it by, when I glanced up a long, sloping driveway and saw Charlie out in his three-car garage with the single-car door wide open. He appeared to be working on something at his work bench.

I flipped a U-turn at the end of the street, and pulled up in front of his house. The architecture was impressive, but hard to pinpoint as far as a style. It was painted a soft tan color with a red-tiled roof. Modern Spanish Colonial came to my mind when I saw it the first time. This time it just seemed to be Southwest with sprawling ranch-style mixed in. But it was one of the few front yards with a sizable patch of green grass which was bordered by a cement curb. Charlie stopped what he was doing and glanced in my direction.

I waved at him, and then got out of my car and trudged my way up the driveway.

"Oh my god, Nola. What are you doing out this way?" Charlie asked in his usual perturbed fashion. He was holding a hacksaw in his hand and appeared to have been cutting through some PVC pipe.

"First of all, I wanted to know if you've heard from your mom. Did you ever try calling her on her cell?"

"She doesn't have a cell phone. Hates modern technology. She'll come home when she's ready to. And for the last time, Nola, it's none of your business."

"Okay, okay, Charlie. But my other reason for dropping by is that I need to finish writing my bios for the community awards article and your mom's is the only one I have left. Since I can't interview her right now, I thought I'd get what I can from you, if that's alright. I need to meet my deadline soon."

"You couldn't call first? Look, I'm right in the middle of something here, Nola. Can't you tell? I'm trying to fix the watering system. Can't we do this later?" Further perturbation had reared its ugly head.

"I just have a few questions. You can work while we talk, okay?"

"Well, crap. Let's get this over with." He put the saw down on the work bench, and then turned around and folded his arms across his chest.

I quickly wrapped up the interview and turned to further inquiry about Myrtle's whereabouts. Charlie was no more forthcoming than before, and he ended up telling me to leave. Again.

* * * *

Driving back into town, I realized it had been more than two hours since I had talked to Mother and told her I'd be coming over there. I made a quick stop back at home to feed the pets, and then headed over to her house.

Mother was already fixing dinner when I arrived.

"I thought we might try the new restaurant," I complained.

"Well, dear, when you didn't show up in two hours I started cooking. That's what I do. We're having beef stew, by the way."

"I know. I could smell it as soon as I came through the door. Smells delicious." That signaled I was resigned to eating in after all. "We can try Picante's some other time."

Seated in our usual spots at the dining room table, we enjoyed our stew and sour dough bread in silence. When I had had my fill, I began relating the day's events to her while she continued eating.

"So, I went on an impromptu ride-along with Officer Frye this morning," I started out.

"That's nice, honey. Was it interesting?"

"Well, he got called to an auto accident scene. Turns out Doctor Barber was apparently run off the road and ended up nose down in the creek."

"Oh, my goodness!"

"He told the first responders that he was headed out to Betty Rayburn's, but Betty said she wasn't expecting him to make a house call."

"So someone tried to harm him? I don't like him that much, but I wouldn't wish him any harm."

"Well, supposedly that's what he said had happened. They're still investigating. The doctor was taken to the hospital in Dowd. At least he was still conscious when the paramedics rescued him."

Mother put down her fork. "Who would do such a thing?"

"No idea. But I came across some interesting information about him." I decided to jump right in. "Did you know he had organized a local marijuana club for the chemo patients?"

She hesitated before answering by picking up her fork again. "Well, yes, but I thought it was a secret. Except that Nellie told me all about it, so I guess it wasn't the best kept secret in town." She forked another bite of stew but held it in the air.

"And you never said anything to me?" I railed.

"Nola, I was asked by Nellie not to tell anyone. Anyway, I thought it was a good thing if it was helping my friends get through their bad times. I didn't think it was important that you should know. Besides, you're a reporter and you might have written a story about it, for all I know. I didn't want to be a traitor to my friends, you know."

"Do you have any idea who knew about it and who was opposed to the club? Anyone who would have gone after Doctor Barber? If you do, you need to report it to Jeff . . . Officer Frye. Or Captain Peachtree. Or someone in authority, for God's sake!" I was incensed.

"Calm down, Nola, and let me think." She finally put the forkful of stew in her mouth.

I tapped my fingers on the table, displaying my impatience.

Finished chewing, she swallowed and then began to speak. "I heard that Myrtle wasn't too fond of the idea. Why, I don't know. Maybe she was afraid her precious son might join the club. Nellie told me that anyone could participate. That they needed volunteers to help with the cultivation out at Archie's place. Apparently, Myrtle had threatened to shut them down, but she never said anything to me about it. Where is she anyway?" she sighed. "Nobody has seen or heard from her in days now."

Obviously, Mother hadn't connected Myrtle with the body parts showing up yet or she would have been more frantic.

"Did you know about her male *friend* in Dowd? Greg Goldberg?" I had decided to lay everything out on the table . . . except for the gruesome stuff.

"You mean Buddy? Yes, sad story. But I'm happy that they found each other again. They say that real love stories never have endings. Don't you believe that, Nola?"

"I don't know, Mom. Mine kinda ended abruptly." A lump suddenly grew in my throat and a tear threatened to fall from my left eye.

"But you still love each other, right?" Mom reached out to pat my hand.

"Of course. We will always have that." I then cleared my throat. "Now, how did we get so far off the subject?"

"What is the subject, anyway?" Lillian asked before taking another bite of bread.

"The marijuana club."

"Oh, right," she said between chews, then swallowed and continued. "Well, that's all I know. Like I said, I'm not opposed to the idea if it helps my friends."

"Wait a minute. You said something about cultivating the marijuana *out* at Archie's place. But he lives here in town, doesn't he?"

"I know that, dear. But he owns some property north of town. He's got some old rundown place that was built by one of the early settlers."

It was becoming obvious to me that I had been away so long that I was no longer a budding tendril in the Cider Crossing grapevine.

"Is it on the road to Betty's place?" I queried.

"I've never seen it, so I'm not sure. But that sounds about right, according to Nellie."

"Hmm. Maybe that's where Doctor Barber was headed when he careened off the road," I mused aloud.

"What? I thought you said he was on his way to see Betty Rayburn. Poor thing, I heard she sprained her ankle. Someone will have to help out at the food closet until she gets better. You know, Nola . . .

"No, Mom, not me. I've got enough on my plate with work and the remodel."

"Enola Gay!" Mom called me by my given name, which my dad had chosen not realizing how inappropriate and embarrassing it would become.

"Mom! I go by Nola now, remember?"

"Oh, good night!" Lillian spat out her signature interjection.

I took another bite of stew, which had turned cold. Mother was poised and waiting for me to retaliate.

Instead, I continued with the Dr. Barber details. "He told the paramedics he was on his way out to Betty's place, but Betty told me she wasn't expecting him. That's why I now think he might have been going out to see Archie and didn't want anyone to know that."

"You're probably right, Nola. But who's going to check on Betty now that Doctor Barber is in the hospital?"

"I should probably go out there myself to see if she needs anything. Maybe tomorrow. I'll call her later."

"Have you talked to Carla lately?" Mother was asking about my friend Pinky who lived up north. We grew up together, but I hadn't seen her since I moved back home. Mother still referred to her by her given name, but I've called her by her nickname—since forever. We're total opposites, however. She's always been a "girlie girl." I, on the other hand, grew up a tomboy. But, we somehow fell into a symbiotic relationship that works for both of us.

"No, not lately, but I should probably call her tonight also. She might even have an idea about who would try to run Doctor Barber off the road. I *have* used her as my sounding board in the past. Yeah, that sounds like a good idea. Note to self—call Pinky."

"Well, good. Help me clear the table, please, and then you'd better get on home."

21

As soon as I got home, I checked on the cat and bird and then grabbed the phone and sat down in my recliner to call Betty.

"Hey, Betty, how are you doing?"

"Hi, Nola. Oh, I'm not sure. I think my ankle is getting worse. It's been harder to get around. I've had to hop along on my good leg and now it's starting to hurt also. I guess I should go see someone. Trouble is, my doctor is in Dowd and I'm not sure how I'll get there. Can't drive myself since it's my right ankle that's sprained. Or broken, heaven forbid. I probably need an x-ray. Sheesh!"

"Okay, I'm coming out there tomorrow. I think my mom still has the crutches my dad used when he broke his leg. I'll pick them up and bring them to you in the morning. Meanwhile, go ahead and call your doctor for an appointment. I can drive you to Dowd, no problem. Plus, I can stop by the hospital and check on Doctor Barber while we're there. That is, if he hasn't been released yet."

"Oh, thank you, Nola. You're so thoughtful and kind."

"Just helping out a friend, Betty. See you tomorrow."

We hung up and I punched in Pinky's number while I made my way to the kitchen to pour a glass of red wine.

"Nola! I was just thinking about you," Pinky answered in amazement.

"Let's have a glass of wine together while we catch up," I suggested as I picked up my goblet and headed back to my recliner.

"I'm right there with you. So, how is everything?"

"Not sure where to begin. How about you and Steve, and Coco, of course? How've you guys been?" Pinky was lucky to have found Steve on her third try at marriage. He doted on her and was able to spoil her rotten with his six-figure income as a financial advisor. I was happy for them.

"Pretty good. Coco is curled up on my lap right now, by the way. So, nothing going on as exciting as when you were here, but hey. Oh, believe it or not, Steve has decided to get fitted for prosthetics. It only took him over twenty years to make that decision, so this oughta be interesting."

"That's fantastic! Guess he finally got tired of wheeling around." Steve had been able to make a successful life for himself despite the fact that he had been injured during his stint in the Army and ended up a double amputee.

"He'll have to do some physical therapy sessions at first, but he's been exercising his arms and upper legs all along, so he should be up and about in no time."

"Well, tell him I wish him success."

"Okay. Your turn," Pinky prompted.

"Let's see. Body parts have been showing up all over town," I reported.

"Body parts? Yuck! Whose are they, and *what* are they?"

"A hand, a foot and a finger. No word yet on who they belong to."

"Nola, I swear, wherever you go, mystery abounds. Are you working the case?"

"Not officially, of course, but I *have* been snooping around."

"As a reporter or a sleuth?"

"Both. It seems that Myrtle Maxwell is missing and then someone may have tried to run Cecil Barber off the road—and succeeded. Not sure if all these incidents are related or not. I'll check with law enforcement again tomorrow to see if there are any developments on any of this." I felt like I was out of breath.

"Sounds like you're right in the thick of things again. Is Doctor Barber okay?"

"I haven't heard anything yet."

"So, how's Mom?" Pinky asked.

"Oh, she's fine. I just had dinner with her tonight. She's still functioning somewhat normally. What about your mom? I haven't seen her out and about lately. I should stop by some time."

"Yeah, she doesn't get out much anymore. Her caregiver does all her shopping for her. I need to get down there to visit. Maybe when Steve gets his legs working we'll make the trip. Love to see *you*, too."

"Oh, I just thought of something else. Doctor Barber has organized a marijuana club for chemo patients and others. Olive Quigley, Harold Raymond,

Nellie Semple and Archie Tanner are the chemo patients. They all seem to be doing really well."

"Really? How are the townspeople taking to all this?"

"Well, it's supposed to be a secret, but you know how the grapevine works around here. Not everyone is thrilled with the idea. Charlie Maxwell's wife, Blanche, told me that Myrtle was extremely opposed to it and threatened to report Doctor Barber to the authorities."

"So, if Myrtle was upset with Doctor Barber she could have been the one who ran him off the road. Only she was already missing, right? I'm confused. I need a timeline." It was apparent that Pinky had already put on her thinking cap.

"Okay. Myrtle's been missing for at least a week. The hand showed up on Wednesday. The foot and finger were discovered on Thursday. The accident occurred just this morning. I was on a ride along with Jeff Frye when that happened. So we rushed to the scene and saw that Doctor Barber's car had careened down the embankment and ended up nose down in the creek."

"Yikes!" Pinky exclaimed.

"I know. He was transported by ambulance to the hospital in Dowd to be checked out. I may be going over there to see how he's doing. Betty Rayburn needs to see her doctor about her injured ankle and I told her I'd drive her. Now, let me tell you about Myrtle's secret affair."

"What? She was having an affair at her age? With who?"

"Her high school sweetheart, Greg Goldberg, who goes by the nickname of Buddy. Apparently, they were an item back then, but when he was drafted and sent to Okinawa they drifted apart. Or, rather, she started dating Ernie Maxwell and ended things with Greg by sending him a "Dear John" letter. He told me he was devastated, but got on with his life and became an attorney. But, they got back together again after Ernie passed away, even though Greg is now married to a woman named Greta. His wife, however, is not in good health. I have talked to Greg twice now, so that's how I know all this. He lives in Dowd. I may want to meet with him also while I'm there."

"Whew! That's a lot of info you've gleaned, Nola. You've definitely met your calling by becoming a reporter."

"I'm not a career reporter, Pinky, I'm only working to help pay for the remodel. I'm retired, remember? But I must have a way of falling into these things. Or maybe they just fall into me. I don't know." I took a sip of wine.

"So . . . Myrtle is missing, body parts are appearing but we don't know whose they are, and someone may have tried to kill Doctor Barber. Hmmm. You've got a mystery on your hands again. I take it you've ruled out Greg, or rather Buddy, from having anything to do with Myrtle's disappearance? I mean, where is she anyway?"

"Buddy said they were supposed to meet last Monday, but she never showed. He called in a missing person report on Thursday after he hoped she would be there on Wednesday instead. He seems genuinely concerned about her," I continued. "Oh, I just thought of something else. Darn. I need to start writing these things down."

"Like a reporter? Okay, let's have it."

"I inadvertently spied Winnie Blankenship and Olive Quigley kissing down by the creek. Almost the same exact place that the doctor took his dive. I thought it was odd, but who am I to judge? So, I tried to get Florence Halladay to spill the beans, but she began playing word games with me. Said they had a secret and that maybe Myrtle was going to tell Winnie's husband about it. She alluded to that being a motive for Myrtle's disappearance. If you ask me, crazy Florence might have something to do with it. Olive revealed to me that Ernie dumped Florence to be with Myrtle, and I don't think she ever got over that. But why would she exact revenge after all these years? Crap! It just seems like everyone's a suspect, damn it!"

"Wait a minute—Ernie once dated Florence?" Pinky asked in disbelief.

"I know, right?"

"Well, have you talked to Winnie or Olive about their relationship?"

"No. I don't know how to approach them about such a delicate subject."

"Right. Well, maybe Winnie and her husband have a marriage of convenience. I mean, he's gone a lot for his job, right? My mom told me that. I always suspected he was leading a double life. Don't know why, just do." I could hear her shuffling about. "Hang on, Coco's gotta go outside."

Pinky's Bichon Frise was her and Steve's only "child" and was as pampered as a dog could be.

While I waited for her to return to the phone, I thought of a few other things to tell her. That reminded me to write everything down next time before I called her.

"Okay, I'm back," Pinky reported once she got back on the phone.

"So, speaking of clandestine affairs, I also spotted Blanche and Jeff being all cozy in front of one of the properties she has listed."

"You're kidding! Jeff and Blanche? They're *both* married, for heaven's sake."

"I'm not sure what that was all about, but I asked my mom about it and she said that Myrtle suspected something was going on with those two and threatened to tell Jeff's wife. Blanche denied the allegation but kept mum about the situation."

"Another motive to make Myrtle disappear? Seems kinda farfetched, if you ask me. I mean, I always thought Jeff was smitten with his wife. Maybe there's a reasonable explanation for Blanche being so secretive. I don't know. Oh my god, Nola. Why are you always surrounded with intrigue?" I could hear her take a sip of her wine.

"My lot in life, I guess," I sighed. "Did I mention the rock being thrown through the office window?"

"What? Uh, no, you did not. When did that happen?"

"Last Thursday night. I'm not sure it's related to all this, but there was a note wrapped around it that said 'Back Off' in all caps. I can't imagine it was meant for me. Maybe Calvin is the target. After all, he's the political and crime reporter, I just write the fluff. I should have him check the police logs prior to the incident to see if there's some connection." Note to self—again.

"Okay, so how many suspects do we have here?" Pinky continued. "Let's see . . . everyone in the pot club, Winnie, Olive, Florence, Blanche, Jeff and . . . what about Charlie? Would he have motive to get rid of his mother? I mean, besides inheriting everything. Oops! I forgot about Ivy. What about Ivy?"

"Both she and Charlie have been interviewed and say they have no clue where their mother is. Well, Charlie claimed he has a suspicion, but wouldn't elaborate other than to imply she's off on some tryst. Little does he know that would have been with Buddy. But, like I said, Buddy swears he doesn't know what happened to her either. Oh, this is so confusing!"

"Well, let's sleep on it and we can have another brain-storming session later on in the week. But let me know if something new turns up in the meantime. Hopefully, Myrtle."

"Will do. Say 'hi' to Steve for me. 'Night."

22

The next morning I called Mother to tell her I would be stopping by to pick up Dad's crutches, if she still had them. She did, and she was glad to hear that I was taking good care of Betty, even though I wouldn't be volunteering at the Pots and Pants place, she added. Mom never missed an opportunity to get her two cents in, I reminded myself, and so I didn't take offense.

On my way out to Betty's I noticed that same pickup parked behind the outbuilding that I'd seen before. So, I decided to pull in and check out what that was all about.

Having parked on the dirt driveway, I walked up to the building and could hear a whirring sound coming from inside. There was no door visible on the front side, so I went around to the back, passing by the rusty old Ford pickup. A large door stood open, and the sound was distinctively louder. The noise being made reminded me of my power saw cutting through wood. Soon the cacophony stopped. Wood dust floated out the door.

"Hello?" I called out.

"Who's out there?" I heard a man's voice shout.

"It's Nola . . . Nola Martin. Is that you, Archie?"

Archie stuck his head out the door and acknowledged me. "What are you doing here, Nola?" he asked suspiciously.

"I was on my way out to Betty Rayburn's and I noticed your pickup. I wondered who was using this place. Sorry for the intrusion. Reporter's curiosity, I guess. So, what are you making in there? Sounded like you were sawing something."

"Yeah, I bought this place for a song about a year ago. If you really must know, I'm building tables for a greenhouse." Dressed in bib overalls, he was standing in the doorway as if guarding what was inside.

"Greenhouse? You mean to grow stuff inside. Like, perhaps, marijuana?" I couldn't help but expose the fact that I knew all about the MJ club.

"What? Hell, no," he retorted.

"Archie, I heard you tell Iris that you don't play with pansies after she told you she saw you buying a grow light at the hardware store. So, why else would you be working on a greenhouse? Hmmm? Besides, I know all about the MJ club and that you are a member," I asserted.

"Okay, fine. But don't be reporting this in the newspaper. We decided to start our own pot farm a while back. Everyone volunteers in some way or another. Oh, hell, come on in," he gestured toward the interior.

I ducked inside and saw an amazing array of greenery accompanied by a distinctively powerful aroma. There were several wooden structures with draining screens on top mounted on cinder blocks for support, and water was still dripping from beneath the plants. Artificial sun lamps hung from the ceiling, and a watering hose was coiled up on the compacted dirt floor. In the corner was a pile of wood and the Skilsaw where Archie had been constructing the additional table. There was also a round thermometer mounted on the wall and a box fan placed strategically in another corner. A potting bench rounded out the greenhouse array.

"Rumor has it that this is the place where Pete Seeger used to brew his hard cider during Prohibition. Ha! We've put a lot of work into it, too."

"Nice, Archie," I commented while still looking around. "Don't worry, I won't tell anyone. Half the town knows, or suspects, anyway."

"It was Doctor Barber's idea. He's been great working with all us chemo patients. I heard he was in the hospital after being run off the road yesterday. I hope he's alright and gets back soon. We need his support."

"I'm planning on going to visit him to find out what happened. I'll let you know how he's doing. Well, I'd better get going. See ya, Archie."

* * * *

I knocked on Betty's front door. "It's Nola," I hollered.

"Come on in, Nola," Betty hollered back.

Entering the front room I found Betty sitting back in her recliner with her right leg raised. It looked swollen. I leaned the crutches nearby. "How are you doing?"

"Not so good. I think it's getting worse every day," she sighed. "I was able to get an appointment, however, for tomorrow afternoon in Dowd."

"Great! I will definitely be able to take you, and also check on Doctor Barber while we're there."

"What a relief! I've got to get back to normal as soon as possible, darn it all!"

"Meanwhile, can I do anything for you while I'm here? Like fix you something to eat?"

"That would be wonderful. A tuna sandwich would be fine. If you can make two, I'll have the other one later. Not much appetite lately, what with all this pain."

"Are you taking pain pills?"

"No, just ibuprofen. Which reminds me, I think it's time for another dose."

"I'll get it. In the kitchen?"

"Let me try hobbling in there on these things," she countered as she reached for the crutches.

Betty was able to get around okay with the mobility aids, so after I fixed her sandwiches, and made sure she was stable, I told her I'd be back at ten the next morning and left.

* * * *

As I was driving back into town, my car started making that peculiar sound again. Okay, fine, I'll stop in at Mac's Auto Repair when I get there—*if* I get there, I warned myself.

Mac's didn't appear to be that busy when I pulled into the driveway. There was only one car in the double bay and two cars in the parking area. Joe,

Mac's only mechanic, was in the bay with his head stuck under the hood of the car he was working on.

Mac Donovan himself came out to greet me. A friend of my dad's, he knew me well. I stepped out of my car, keys in hand.

"Hey, Nola, what can I do for you?"

"My car is making a funny noise up front and it's scaring me. I have to drive to Dowd tomorrow, and I don't want to break down out there in the middle of nowhere."

Mac chuckled briefly. "I'll pull her on into the empty bay and take a look. Shouldn't take that long," he assured as he held out his hand.

"Thanks, Mac." I handed him the keys, grabbed my purse, and then went inside to take a seat in the customer waiting area.

While I was biding my time, I thought about calling Buddy to see if I could meet up with him while in Dowd. But I didn't have his number in my cell, so I decided to call him once I got home. I picked up a Motor Trend magazine instead and began flipping through the pages.

Mac finally came in to report that it was my alternator belt making the noise and it needed to be replaced. "I'm pretty sure I have one in stock, so we'll get you going in no time."

He was back inside in about fifteen minutes, after I noticed he had parked my car next to one of the others outside.

I paid him and thanked him again. As I was heading out the door he mentioned that he was still waiting for Myrtle to pick up her car.

"I've been trying to get ahold of her, so if you see her would you remind her that her car is ready?"

"What? Myrtle's car is here?"

"Yeah, the tan one parked next to yours out there," he confirmed.

"How long has it been here, I mean, when did she bring it in?" I was perplexed. I realized I had failed to recognize it even though I had read the description in the missing person report. Mac's was the last place anyone would think to look.

"About a week ago, maybe longer. I'd have to check my invoices."

This startling bit of information cast a whole new light on the situation. I would have to rethink everything, so I decided not to go into detail with Mac just yet.

"Okay, I'll see if I can find her," I stated. Of course, the true meaning of that statement was totally lost on Mac.

23

Bursting through my side door, I threw my purse down and picked up the phone to call Jeff. No answer. Darn. He probably wasn't on duty that day. Or else . . . maybe another secret rendezvous?

My two housemates were starting to fuss. Bertie was singing and Flossie was mewing. Both wanting attention and food. But I had to get this newfound information to someone first.

I rang the police station, knowing the number by heart, and asked to speak with Captain Peachtree.

"Captain? This is Nola Martin. I know you're aware that Myrtle Maxwell is missing and I just found out that she had dropped her car off at Mac's Auto Repair over a week ago. So, she obviously didn't drive somewhere like we all thought."

"Okay, I'll have Officer Frye go talk to Mac. By the way, I received some preliminary info on the hand that was found. No DNA report yet, but forensics show that it was severed with some kind of saw, based on the striations, as they put it. No word yet on the foot or the finger. I'll let you know when I hear more.

"Hmm. This is all very disturbing. I don't want to point any fingers, no pun intended, but I've encountered two people recently who were wielding saws. Would that help? I mean, maybe you could rule them out or something. I don't know. I'm still trying to put two and two together."

"Who were they?" Peachtree sounded curious.

I hesitated at first, and then finally replied, "Charlie Maxwell and Archie Tanner. On separate occasions, of course, and with different kinds of saws. It's probably nothing, or just a coincidence. Maybe I shouldn't have said anything."

"No, no, every little bit helps. Thanks, Nola," he said before he hung up.

I fed my little monsters, and then decided to let Pinky in on the latest. I obviously wasn't going to get any work done at the office today. But I could finish the flower show story at home once I got the results from Florence. But first things first.

"Pinky, I already have an update for you," I announced the second she answered her phone.

"Already? Good. I've been working on theories in my head. Let's have it," she jumped right in.

"Well, my car's been making a strange noise, so I took it in to Mac's today. Long story short, he fixed the problem."

"What does that have to do with anything?"

"I'm getting to that. As I was leaving, he told me that Myrtle had left her car there a week or so ago. Said he'd been trying to get ahold of her. He asked me to remind her if I saw her. Since her car wasn't in her garage, everyone was assuming she had driven it somewhere. '*Where*' was the question, now it's not. I'm so scared that something has happened to her."

"So am I, now," Pinky concurred.

"I called Captain Peachtree to let him know this, and he updated me on the hand that was found. Forensics described that it was severed with some kind of saw. Coincidentally, I recently witnessed Charlie and Archie both using saws, which I told the Captain. Egads! What am I doing? I'm not a detective. Or am I?"

"Sure you are. Amateur, maybe, but you helped solve the gypsy mystery, remember?"

"Of course. How can I forget that? I almost got myself killed."

"I'm so glad you didn't," she commiserated with a laugh. "So, I'm thinking that Charlie may have something to do with his mom's disappearance. Or Blanche for that matter. Maybe they're in this together. They both have the most to gain. And I'm sure Blanche would love to have her mother-in-law out of the picture. But still, I'm not so sure either one of them could do something that horrific."

"I know. I keep going in circles in my head also," I agreed.

"Well, with all this new info in mind, I've got to run to the grocery store and then start preparing dinner when I get back. Later." And she was off.

I'd better check in with Cal was my next thought—or I'd never hear the end of it.

"Cal, it's Nola. I'll be working at home tonight, and tomorrow I'm driving Betty Rayburn over to Dowd to have her ankle looked at. Sorry I haven't been around much, but I'll make it up to you on Wednesday," I apologized.

"Criminy, Nola. We've got to get this edition under control. Good thing Julius won't be back until this weekend. I'd hate for him to see us drowning in chaos," Cal complained.

"Chaos? C'mon, Cal, it'll be fine. Besides, maybe we'll have some news on the body parts soon. That'll be sensational, don't ya think?"

"Whatever, Nola. I've got to get back to work." He hung up.

Next, I called Florence to get the final results of the flower show competition. She told me to meet her at the botanical society clubhouse.

24

As I pulled up in front of the botanical society house, another car pulled up behind me. Assuming it was Florence, I glanced into my rearview mirror and recognized Winnie instead.

We greeted each other on the sidewalk. "I'm meeting Florence here," I explained.

"Oh. Well, come on in. I have a key in case Florence isn't here yet," Winnie invited.

The door was locked, so we knew she hadn't arrived. "Maybe she's walking over. It's been such a beautiful day," Winnie sang out.

Once inside, we pulled out folding chairs from the meeting table and sat facing each other. I noticed that all of the entries were still on display. Some of the plants looked a little droopy, so I was hoping Florence was coming over to tend to them.

"So, what brings you here?" Winnie asked.

"I need the results of the flower show competition so I can finish my story before the paper goes to print."

"Right. Florence is the only one of us with that information. She guards it with her life, believe it or not. Whatever makes her feel important, I guess," Winnie added. "Plus, she's waiting for the ribbons to get here so she can hand them out on Thursday." She glanced toward the front door.

"Are you expecting someone? Olive, for instance?" I teased.

"No. Why would you say that?" she snapped back.

"I saw the two of you down by the creek the other day, that's all."

"Well, we like to go wading when it's warm outside," she covered.

"I'm not judging, but it looked like you were doing a lot more than wading."

"What? Well, for goodness sake, what are you implying?" Winnie's face was turning a bit red.

"Look, Winnie, it's okay. So you two have a special relationship. Lots of people do. It's no big deal."

"Well, in a small town like ours it's a bigger deal than you think."

"Really? I guess you're right. Cider Crossing is somewhat behind the times, isn't it? What about your husband? Does he know?"

"Donald? Donald could care less. He has his own life."

"So how is it that you've been married all these years? And why did you get married in the first place?" I was becoming more and more intrigued with her story.

"My parents forced me into it. I was in my thirties by then and still living at home. They gave me an ultimatum: either get a job or get married. They introduced me to Donald, who they knew through business connections. Although he was from out of town, they insisted he was a 'good catch' because he made good money. Salary *and* commission for him doing his sales job."

"And so Donald proposed?"

"After a few dates he said he wanted to get married right away. Even though he's about ten years younger than I am, he wasn't that good looking, but it didn't matter to me. I've never been attracted to men anyway. On our wedding night I told him point blank that I wouldn't be engaging in any physical activities. I was shocked when he was relieved. That's when he told me he was gay and only needed to get married to please his employer. Remember this was almost forty years ago. We've actually had a very pleasant marriage. I'm sure he has a boyfriend in every town he visits for his job, but I'm happy for him. So, it works for both of us. Olive and I have been carrying on for years now. And we're very happy, too."

Winnie pushed her chair back and stood up.

"Does anyone in town know about you guys? I mean, I'm sure there are suspicions. Has anyone said anything?" My curiosity was pushing me further.

"Not really. Myrtle knows, and she's fine with it. She lets us use her place when she's out of town. We can't hang out at Olive's overnight because Old Man Tucker next door would have a cow, and so would *my* neighbors. Charlie knows because she told him we'd be watching her house every time she goes out of town so he doesn't have to. He was fine with that. Acting as her caretaker is beneath him, you know," she ended with a laugh.

"Myrtle is still missing, you know," I reported.

"That is so strange. Olive and I didn't realize she was gone until recently or we would have been over there checking on the house and feeding the cat."

"Well, Charlie and I were over there the other day. I hope he's still feeding the cat. He hasn't said anything to you?"

"Nope. Not a word."

The sound of footsteps approaching on the front porch caught our attention.

"That must be Florence. I'd better do what I came here for and get on home. It was good talking to you, Nola," she smiled. "Thank you for understanding."

"Of course. Same to you, Winnie."

25

Florence had provided me with the list of winners, but only after making me swear that I wouldn't reveal the results until after the presentation get-together on Thursday night. I assured her that having the information early would allow me to be able to finish the story on time, and I promised to keep her confidence until the Friday paper was delivered. Sheesh! You'd think she was in charge of the Oscars.

I decided to head over to the office after all. After reviewing the results, I would need to rewrite some of the cutlines for the photos to designate the winners. And I'd already uploaded the photos to my office computer.

I was heading back on Birch Street when I saw two people standing in front of the cottage that was for sale. This time it was Jeff and his wife, Carol, and they were holding hands. Jeff wasn't in uniform. This seemed peculiar, considering I had seen Jeff with Blanche at the same location a few days before, but I drove on past without them noticing me. As I turned right at the next corner, I passed by Blanche in her Caddy as she turned left onto Birch. She didn't even notice me either. This could get interesting, I predicted, but I had work to do.

Cal's car wasn't in the parking lot. Probably out on some assignment. I couldn't keep track of his schedule or what he did half the time, but I was pretty sure he hadn't left for the day.

Letting myself into the office, and locking the door behind me, I got right down to work. I was almost finished with the task when there was a knock at the door. Glancing out the window, I saw a car parked next to mine that I didn't recognize. It wasn't dark yet, but I was still on edge after the rock throwing incident.

I carefully approached the windowed front door only to see Jeff standing outside. Thank goodness it was someone I trusted.

"Hi, Jeff," I greeted him after unlocking and opening the door.

"Hey, Nola. I saw your car parked out front and thought I should stop by and bring you up to speed on the latest."

"Okay . . . come on in. Is this about the flying rock?"

"Uh, no, we still don't know what that was all about. No further incidents though, right? Nothing else strange going on?"

"Nothing that I know of. So, what do you have for me?"

"It's about the foot that was found down by the tracks. Lab determined it had been buried there for some time due to decomp. Also, they could tell by the condition that it appeared to have been caught in some kind of trap, possibly a crude bear trap. I vaguely remember something like that happening years ago to some homeless guy. It was before my time as a cop," he clarified. "Anyway, I heard his friends had carried him all the way into town without his foot looking for help. When authorities went searching the area near their campsite, there was no sign of any trap or other makeshift device, let alone the foot. Those spring-loaded traps have been illegal for over twenty years here, but people used to set them out down by the tracks to catch skunks, coyotes, raccoons, you name it. Maybe they still do. Come to think of it, I haven't seen many wild animals roaming around lately. At least not the furry kind," he laughed. "So, it could be that guy's foot that was dug up, or someone else's from a while ago. Whatever, Captain Peachtree doesn't see it as a current need for investigation, but someone will still be looking into it."

"What a relief it isn't recent," was all I could think to say.

"Well, I just thought you would like to know," Jeff said as he turned to leave.

"Oh, I almost forgot, Jeff. I found out that Myrtle's car has been sitting in Mac's parking lot for over a week now. I tried calling you to let you know, but you didn't pick up so I called Captain Peachtree instead. That means she never left down, right? At least in her own vehicle."

He turned back around. "That's interesting. Don't know why we didn't spot the car, but we were all assuming she had left town."

"Has anyone heard from the detectives assigned to the case?"

"I haven't, but I'll check with Captain Peachtree and let you know if he's heard anything. By the way, I think the Captain is interested in you," he divulged before turning to leave again.

"What? Wait a minute, Jeff. Didn't I just see you and your wife about an hour ago standing in front of that house for sale on Birch? Are you interested in buying it?"

"Yeah. I wanted to surprise Carol, so Blanche showed me the house first. I've already started the paperwork. It'll be our first house. We've been wanting to start a family, so Carol is thrilled to have a yard for kids to play in. Plus, we can finally adopt a dog from the rescue shelter."

"I'm so happy for you guys. She must still be over there looking around and planning her decorating scheme."

"No, I just dropped her off at work. She's been working the night shift at Ernie's. I was headed back to the apartment when I noticed your car."

"You are an exemplary policeman, Officer Frye. You'll soon be promoted to sergeant, I predict."

"Thanks, Nola. I passed the test and I'm reachable on the list. Hopefully it won't be long. Okay, later." And he was out the door.

As soon as he drove off, I processed the new information. Okay, so I was wrong about Blanche and Jeff having a fling. This also left no motive for Blanche to be revengeful toward her mother-in-law for accusing her of infidelity, since it wasn't true. I'll need to bring Pinky up-to-date later tonight about both the foot and the non-affair, I entered onto my mental checklist. Oh, right, add to that the Olive and Winnie explanation, too.

One by one, I seemed to be eliminating suspects in Myrtle's disappearance. That only left a few.

26

Cal hadn't returned by the time I left for home, so I locked up behind myself. I had left a note on his desk suggesting that he scan the recent police logs to see if there was any disgruntled citizen who could have thrown the rock through the window. I knew it would be a long shot, but it wouldn't hurt checking. As I worded it in the note, it was just a suggestion.

The streets were quiet as I drove the short distance to my house, and twilight had set in. Must be dinner time, I reckoned.

After doing my usual routine with the pets, I made myself something to eat. It dawned on me that, other than my morning coffee and English muffin, I hadn't had anything to eat all day. With another microwaved meal down the hatch, I poured myself a glass of wine and sat down to call Pinky again.

"Twice in one day? This story must be moving fast," was her way of answering the phone.

"I learned three more things this afternoon, and I needed to confer with my co-detective," I joked.

"Okay, shoot."

"First, Jeff Frye stopped by the office to let me know that the foot is old, according to forensics. At least not a recent injury. He remembered an incident some time ago where a homeless guy lost his foot in a spring-loaded trap. Anyway, it can't belong to Myrtle. I'm sure of that and relieved as well."

"Me, too, but the poor homeless guy. Whew!"

"Next, I was able to talk to Winnie by chance when I ran into her at the botanical society. She told me all the details about Donald, her husband. Long story, but apparently they're both gay and have a mutual understanding. She assured me that their marriage was fine. So, if Myrtle was threatening to inform him about Olive, that wouldn't have made a difference. Therefore, Winnie and Olive would have no reason to stifle Myrtle. Does that make sense?"

"Sure. Like I told you, I thought he was living a double life. I just didn't factor in that Winnie was okay with that. So cross those suspects off the list. What else?"

"Another affair to discount . . . Jeff and Blanche. I spotted Jeff and his wife Carol today in front of the same house I had seen him with Blanche the other day, so I had to ask when he came by the office. Turns out he was scoping out the house as a possible purchase and surprise for Carol. Blanche had just been showing him the house that day. That's all there was to it. They're buying the house, by the way. Once again, Myrtle blabbing to Carol that her husband was seeing Blanche would have only thrown a monkey wrench into the surprise, I guess. But that didn't happen, and Jeff had no motive anyway because it wasn't true."

"Okay. So who does that leave now?" Pinky mused.

"Well, the other members of the pot club, Harold, Nellie and Archie, could have motives to silence Myrtle, but I'm not sensing that. I'm still suspicious of Florence though. And I haven't ruled out Charlie just yet. But, then again, all of these people could have ulterior motives I haven't considered. Or, it could be someone else entirely. Someone we haven't even thought of yet. See? Is this what they call a conundrum? Or, what was it Churchill called it? 'A riddle wrapped in a mystery inside an enigma.' That's what we're dealing with here."

"Alright. I'll keep my thinking cap on and call you if I come up with any new ideas. Maybe I'll talk to some of my connections down there. It's hard to immerse myself in this mystery being so far away, but I'll try."

"Thanks, Pinky. You're a great partner in crime," I chuckled. "Only we're not the perpetrators, are we? Oh, and don't forget I'm driving Betty over to Dowd tomorrow, so I probably won't be home 'til early evening. My cell's not always reliable. And thanks again for being there."

"Nola. I'm always here for you, you know that. Gotta go."

As soon as we hung up, I remembered what I thought I heard Jeff mutter about Captain Peachtree as he was leaving. I'd have to share that little tidbit with Pinky next time.

By then it was after eight o'clock, but I dialed the office anyway to see if Cal had come back from wherever. He answered on the first ring, sounding different and jovial. When I referenced the note I had left him, he kindly explained that he didn't have time at the moment, but he would look into that the next day, if possible. If he couldn't, then I'd check the police logs myself. But when would *I* have the time for that? I was sure I'd be out-of-town most of the following day. Oh, well.

But that reminded me of something I hadn't done yet. Two things, actually.

27

I needed to call the hospital in Dowd to see if Dr. Barber was still a patient there. I also needed to call Buddy to see if we could meet up some time tomorrow.

I sat down at my desk to look up the number on my computer for Dowd Medical Center, and then talked to the first person who answered the phone. He transferred me to the second floor nurse's station where, I assumed, Dr. Barber was being treated. The nurse who took the transferred call couldn't give me any specifics about his condition, but was allowed to impart that he hadn't been released as of yet. This was both good and bad news. "Good" because I planned to visit him there, "bad" because his injuries must have been greater than I had hoped.

I tried Buddy's home number next. He answered right away by pronouncing my name with a sigh of relief. He must have seen my name on his caller ID, I assumed.

"Hi, Buddy. I don't really have any new information on Myrtle's whereabouts, but I'm coming into Dowd tomorrow and wondered if we could get together somehow. Maybe lunch?" I didn't want to tell him I found her car. I'd rather do that in person.

"Let me check my schedule," he replied. I could hear the sound of clacking on a keyboard. "Okay, I'm free all afternoon, as it appears. Greta's in-home care person will be here to look after her, so I'm available whenever you are. It'll be nice for us to meet in person. There's a great Chinese restaurant that just opened up here called Chin's. That is, if you like chow mein."

"Love it. I'll call you when I get there."

"Let me give you my cell number, just in case I'm not at home." He rattled off the number as I searched my desk for a scrap of paper to write it down on.

"I look forward to seeing you tomorrow. Night, Buddy."

28

Tuesday morning I showered and dressed in black slacks and a lightweight gray jacket. The weather had cooled down considerably. When I looked out my kitchen window, I spotted what appeared to be rain clouds in the distance to the West. I hoped it wasn't raining in Dowd. But, then again, we could use some rain here in Cider Crossing.

I stopped to fill up my gas tank, ran out to pick up Betty by ten and then headed back to town to get on the highway leading straight to Dowd.

Betty seemed in good spirits knowing she would finally be treated for her injury. She said she needed to get back to work at the food and clothes closet as soon as possible. Meanwhile, she had been able to recruit a few temporary volunteers.

"This is so desolate out here," Betty observed as we drove through a southern stretch of the Mojave Desert.

"I know," I agreed. "It doesn't look like there's any life out there, but there is. Desert tortoises, for one. It's eerie, but interesting at the same time. There's a whole ecosphere going on out there—or whatever it's called. It's just not obvious to people as they're driving along."

"I'm sure they don't want us to find them, huh?" she added. "The creatures, that is."

"Yeah, but they're probably hiding in plain sight," I concluded. Like maybe the person responsible for Myrtle vanishing into thin air? Now, there's a thought—a very possible one.

"You mean like camouflage," Betty confirmed.

"Something like that. Oh, I heard there is a group of volunteers who go out there to fill up small watering holes for all the inhabitants. I think that's very humane of them."

"Yes, it is. Especially since we haven't had that much rain lately. I know a few of those guys. Good people."

"Speaking of rain, I noticed some clouds to the West this morning, but now they're gone. Rats! I was hoping they were coming our way."

"That would have been nice," Betty concurred, yawned, and then leaned back on the headrest and closed her eyes.

I drove on silently the rest of the way to Dowd.

* * * *

I pulled into the medical complex shortly before noon, and assisted Betty into her doctor's office. She assured me it would be a while since she was going to ask that x-rays be taken. Since the hospital was right next door, I decided to drop in on Dr. Barber first, and then meet Buddy at the Chinese restaurant afterwards. I told Betty my plans and for her to text me when she was ready to go home.

It took me a few minutes to locate Dr. Barber's room, after having to wend my way through a maze of hallways.

He was sitting up in bed with his lunch tray in front of him.

"Nola? Fancy meeting you here," he quipped. "What are you doing in Dowd?" He took a bite of mashed potatoes and put his fork down.

"Visiting you, of course." I had decided against mentioning Betty, so I continued, "I was on a ride-along with Officer Frye when you had your accident. I'm glad you're okay—or at least I'm assuming you are."

"Yeah. I keep telling them to release me, but they keep running tests. Damn medical field. I'm a doctor, for Christ's sake. I know what I'm doing."

"What are they saying about you being able to go home?" I asked.

"Another day at least. I feel fine, by the way."

"That was a close call. Do you remember anything? Like what actually happened?"

"I was quizzed by several law enforcement officials and I told them all the same thing—someone tried to run me off the road. And they succeeded."

"Did you get a look at the vehicle?"

"Nah. It happened so fast."

I didn't want to bring up the suspicion the responders had that he had been drinking, but then he did it for me.

"Alcohol test came back negative. I *told* them I hadn't been drinking. I *never* drink and drive. That's why I always *walk* over to Hernando's," he explained.

"Well, I hope they find out who hit you. I mean, who would do such a thing? And, why you?"

"Everyone has enemies. Believe me. Even you, I suppose. Like Winston Churchill said, *'If you have enemies that means you've stood up for something in your life.'* That's not a direct quote. Or maybc it was Mark Twain who said that. I don't remember."

"So what have *you* stood up for?" I prodded, hoping he'd confess to the marijuana club.

"I always stand up for what's right. And this hospital food is disgusting." He pushed his tray aside.

I thought I would let the cat out of the baggie, so to speak. "I heard about the marijuana club, by the way. I think it's great that you're helping people like that. Very honorable and brave."

"Well, thank you, Nola. I don't know who told you, but I don't care. It needed to be done. But there *are* people who disagree, of course."

"For instance?" I pushed.

"Myrtle Maxwell, for one. Mostly the old-timers around town. Which is funny because they're the ones who run the risk of getting some sort of cancer."

"She's still missing, you know—Myrtle, that is," I informed him. "And I heard about her objection to your enterprise."

"Enterprise? We're not doing it to make money. It's to help people who are suffering from the side effects of chemotherapy, that's all."

A nurse stepped in to take his vitals, so we curtailed our conversation until she left.

"So Myrtle couldn't have been the one to run you off the road. She's nowhere to be found and I discovered that her car has been at Mac's for over a week now. It's all very strange."

"Yes, indeed," he agreed. "That is strange."

"By the way, have you heard about the body parts showing up all over town?" I asked, changing the subject.

"You mean the hand?" he confirmed.

"Yes, that and a foot and a finger. The hand was missing a finger, but the other finger is not a match, apparently. And the foot was thought to be caught in a trap some time ago. Talk about *more* strange," I declared.

"Where was the finger found, may I ask?"

"At the community park. Some German tourists found it sitting on top of the monument dedicated to Cider Crossing and took it to the police station."

"Oh, my goodness! That's where Tommy the Tree Trimmer had his accident. Tom Ballard. He was using his chainsaw when it kicked back and then it came back down and hit his hand. His finger must have flown off somewhere. Stupid kid wasn't wearing gloves. He panicked, but was still able to drive himself to QuikMed. I was there filling in at the time. Too late to reattach the finger now, I'm afraid. But I treated him as best I could. He's fine now. That was several weeks ago, if I recall."

"How awful. But I'm sure the finger didn't land perfectly on top of the marker. Someone must have put it there. Probably kids, we think. Well, that rules out any connection to the foot. Which, it turns out, is way older than a few weeks. I still haven't heard much about the hand yet, however. This is still creepy."

"What's creepy is being in the hospital," Cecil Barber complained.

"Well, hopefully you'll be going home soon," I reassured him. "Now, *I'd* better be going."

I made my way back downstairs and stopped in the lobby to check my phone which had the ringer turned off. No text from Betty yet, so I called Buddy's cell phone to get directions to Chin's and told him I was on my way.

It only took me ten minutes to get there. The restaurant was located in a brand new shopping center and looked very inviting. A car pulled up next to mine in the parking lot and the man who emerged was the spitting image of the guy in the yearbook photo. Older, of course, but still distinguished looking.

"Buddy?" I asked as I left my vehicle.

"Nola?" he said as he approached me with a smile. He even gave me a hug, which was unexpected.

"So good to finally meet you, Buddy."

"You too, Nola."

Cordial greetings aside, we entered the restaurant and were seated promptly.

The décor of the new restaurant was astounding. Large, paper umbrellas in pastel colors were propped over each table. And the gentle sound of a waterfall could be heard in the background, providing a relaxing atmosphere.

"I'm so glad you picked this place, Buddy. It's lovely."

"Glad you like it, Nola."

We studied our menus and then the waiter came to take our orders. I wanted to order a bit of everything, but I settled on egg foo yung, chow mein and fried rice. Buddy ordered the moo shu pork.

"So, I'm sorry I don't have any good news about Myrtle, but I don't have any bad news either. Except that her car has been discovered at an auto repair shop in Cider Crossing," I revealed. I wasn't about to mention the body parts—or at least the hand and finger.

"What? That means she never left town, I guess. But where the heck is she then? This doesn't sound good, Nola. I'm afraid something bad has happened to her and there's nothing I can do about it."

"It's not on you, Buddy," I tried to convince him.

"I know that, but I really care about her. And I'm so glad we rekindled our relationship after all these years. At least I'll always be grateful for that."

"Of course you will," I concurred.

"You know, I saved every love letter she ever sent me when I was stationed on Okinawa. That is, except the last one, the Dear John letter." He paused to clear his throat. "I was so crushed to hear she was marrying Ernie Maxwell. I threw all the envelopes away, but not the letters. They were all I had left of her. Dear 'B' she called me back then."

"Do you still have them?" I asked.

"Well, yes and no. When Greta and I got married I thought it might be a good idea to get rid of them before she found them. Don't get me wrong, I love my wife. It's just that what Myrtle and I had will always be special. I had been keeping her letters in a shoe box up on the bedroom closet shelf. Anyway, I knew I couldn't part with them totally, so I asked Bert Pettis if he would keep them for me. He had always been sympathetic about my situation because he had been in the military also. Only he was one of the ones who actually experienced combat. Came back with a severe case of PTSD. I'm surprised cutting up meat didn't freak him out."

"Yeah. I remember him acting rather strange when Mother would take me with her to pick up pork chops or a rump roast. He didn't talk much. Was kinda curt and somewhat rude. I didn't like him, but I was only a little kid at the time."

"I should probably get my shoe box back from Iris, now that Bert is gone. I guess I'll have to call her. That means I'll also have to run over to Cider Crossing to pick the box up. I haven't been there in ages. Both my parents have been gone for a while now, and I don't have any siblings or relatives still living there, so I haven't had a reason to return. Hopefully, Myrtle will have resurfaced by then and we can see each other. Or, if not, you and I could meet up again. Your turn to pick the restaurant." He leaned back as the waiter delivered our meals.

He seemed to have relaxed somewhat by then. Maybe he had resigned himself to realizing that Myrtle may never be found in his lifetime. He must have been familiar with the Rosie Vasquez story from his generation. Ten years is a long time for a body to go undiscovered.

29

"There she is, Miss America," Bertie sang out in his guttural tenor voice as I entered my house through the side door.

For some reason, on the long drive back home from Dowd, it had dawned on me that Dr. Barber had never been considered a suspect. Just because someone may have gone after him, doesn't automatically make him innocent. That could have been someone seeking revenge. After all, several people had now told me that Myrtle was out to get him. Maybe he got to her first.

Betty had texted me just as Buddy and I were finishing our meal together. He had offered to pay for our lunch, so I thanked him as we said our good-byes and then I hurried off to pick her up and drive her back home.

It was during that boring drive when Betty had mentioned how several people in town had taken a dislike to Dr. Barber. She wasn't the first one to tell me that. Of course, that's what started me thinking. Bad news.

The good news was that Betty's ankle wasn't broken after all, just badly sprained. She would have to stay off of it for another week or so because she was told that the older we get the longer it takes to heal. *Tell me about it.*

Finally home again myself, I ran through my routine of evening chores, before I finally noticed that the message light on my phone was blinking relentlessly.

I had two messages: one each from my two children. They both said they were just checking in. Family wavelength in action, they always seemed to call me around the same time.

First, I called Mother to tell her I was home and that Betty would be fine. Then I called each of my kids back and brought them up to date without going into a lot of detail. They had busy lives themselves and didn't need to be involved in our small town goings on. We all agreed we needed to see each other soon, and said our good-byes.

I headed into the kitchen and checked inside the refrigerator for something to fix for dinner later. It was almost five o'clock by then. Nothing appealed to me, so I thought I'd take a run up to the local grocery store. Gray's Grocers was only a few minutes' drive away.

Another plus, or minus, to living in a small town is that you can hardly go anywhere without running into someone you know. That seemed to be the case at Gray's.

As soon as I grabbed my shopping cart and started wheeling down the first aisle, I ran into Archie. His cart was filled with charcoal briquettes, steaks, ground beef, hamburger buns, pickles, potato chips and other items related to some kind of party or gathering.

"Hey, Archie," I greeted him. "Excuse my noticing, but it looks like you might be having a barbecue."

"How'd you guess?" he chuckled. "Yeah, the club is having a get-together this Sunday at Harold's house. He just bought a new barbecue. You're welcome to come, if you want. We wanted to celebrate Doctor Barber being back home. So glad he's alright."

"I'm sorry. I was going to let you know that, but I just got home a little while ago."

"That's okay, Nola. Nellie called to check on him this afternoon and he told her they're releasing him tomorrow. Harold is going to go pick him up," he informed me.

"Well, I probably won't make it, but we'll see."

"Hey, bring your mom if you do. She knows everyone who's going to be there."

"Like I said, we'll see. Well, I've gotta get to shopping. Thanks for the invite, Archie."

I wheeled on down the aisle, still not sure what I wanted for dinner. Maybe bacon and eggs? Maybe a Caesar salad? Maybe fish and chips? Ideas kept churning through my stomach when I turned into the next aisle. And there was Iris.

She didn't notice me at first. She had her head stuck inside a door of the frozen food section that I was about to peruse.

As I approached her, I glanced inside her shopping cart and saw two huge bottles of bleach next to some paper towels and a few other food items and some produce.

"Hi, Iris," I interrupted.

She glanced at me through the glass door and made a face. Grabbing a few boxes of frozen dinners, she turned and placed them in her cart.

"Nola. Shopping for your mother?" was her snooty reply.

"No, but it looks like *you're* going on a cleaning frenzy," I observed.

"Well, if you really must know, Bert was a pack rat, and his den, or as he called it, his 'man cave,' was a pig sty. I've had tons of cleaning to do lately. He left me with a lot of chores still undone. Typical of him. He was never one to help out around the house," she complained.

"I'm sorry to hear that, Iris. I know it's been hard on you. It took me quite a while to adjust to losing my husband, too." I thought I was being empathetic, but her response changed my stance.

"Brute. That's what he was. I don't miss him at all," she claimed with a huff.

"Surely you don't mean that, Iris. You knew he had psychological problems stemming from his tour in Viet Nam. Yet, you still married him. He must have had *some* redeeming qualities you were attracted to. I think you are still caught up in the grieving process. Of the five stages, maybe you're stuck in the anger stage." I paused, and then qualified my advice by adding, "I'm no psychologist, but just think about it, okay?"

Iris just stared at me, as if she was thinking—or not. I took that as my cue to leave her alone.

With that, I pushed on without another word.

Traveling up and down several more aisles I finally had sufficient items in my basket to give me enough to choose from for my meal that night.

After checking out, I wheeled my groceries out to the parking lot and stowed them in the back. As I got into my car, I noticed Bert's red pickup parked on the next row over.

30

After I finished eating, I remembered I had a couple of new items of interest to report to Pinky. Not much, however, but I wanted to keep her apprised, nonetheless.

"Hey, Pinky, I'm back from Dowd," I greeted her.

"Oh, good, I was wondering if I would hear from you tonight," she replied.

"Not much to tell, but I did learn from Doctor Barber that the finger probably belongs to Tom Ballard, a tree trimmer. So that just leaves the hand. Oh, yeah, and the doctor will be coming home tomorrow. Which reminds me . . . I'm thinking he could be a suspect, too. I mean, I ruled him out because of his humanitarian qualities and also because I assumed he was also being targeted due to his accident. Betty had mentioned on the ride home that he wasn't that well-liked. And she's not the first one I've heard that from. Give it some thought and let me know what you think, okay?"

"Well, it's a distinct possibility. His motive being that Myrtle was his nemesis. He probably had the means and opportunity, being a doctor. I don't know. Let me think about it. But I hope it's not him, for some reason."

"Me, too," I agreed.

"Okay. What about Buddy? Did you get to meet him?"

"Yes. We met at a new Chinese restaurant there and had a nice visit. He's a good looking man, and very sweet. But I think he may be resigned to never seeing Myrtle again—and that scares me. Not that he had anything to do with her missing, but I think he realizes that the more time that passes, the less hope there is of her still being alive. I do too, unfortunately."

"That's too bad. After all these years he'd be losing her for a second time. And you said his wife may be gone soon also. Poor Buddy."

"I know. I feel so sorry for him. He told me that Bert Pettis had been keeping all of Myrtle's love letters for him—except for the last one, of course, which was the opposite of a love letter. The reason was that he didn't want his wife to find them. Anyway, he may be coming over here to get them back. If Myrtle is truly gone, I think he'll want to read them all again in her memory.

"Of course, he'll have to deal with grumpy Iris—speaking of whom, I ran into her at Gray's a little while ago. Strange woman. She told me she had to clean up all of Bert's messes, which explained the bleach and paper towels in her basket. Then, she called him a 'brute' and said she doesn't miss him in the least. Nice wife, don't you think?"

"I never liked her," Pinky noted. "My mom was friends with her in high school, but they drifted apart after graduation. Thank goodness! We'd run into her time and again around town, but she never came over to our house, that I know of."

"I don't like her either. A lot of people don't. She always carries that air of arrogance about her. Bert must have rubbed off on her. He wasn't an outwardly friendly man. Buddy said Bert came back from Viet Nam with a severe case of PTSD. Maybe Iris was the only woman he could find to marry him. They never had any kids, which tells me they hadn't been that close . . . if you get my drift."

"I never had any kids either, Nola, but that doesn't mean . . .

"Yeah, but you were only married for ten minutes each the first two times. I'm just glad you finally found Steve, even though your biological clock had stopped ticking by then . . . I'm sorry."

"No, Nola, you're right. At least we have Coco, and Steve and I couldn't be happier with each other."

"Speaking of relationships . . . Captain Peachtree asked me out to lunch the other day. I declined because I had work to do, but I took a raincheck. Then, a few days later, Jeff mumbled something to me about the captain being interested in me. Or, at least I think that's what he said. I don't know about this. I mean, I still don't think I'm ready for someone new in my life yet. What do you think?"

"You already know what I think. Get out there, Nola. Go to lunch with Captain Peachtree. Socialize more."

"You know what? I don't even know his first name. I'll have to ask Cal. Or maybe he's been mentioned in an article before. Both law enforcement and emergency responders don't like to give out their first names, you know. I'll see what I can find out."

"So you'll go to lunch after all? Whoopee!"

"Not so fast. We'll see," I countered. But strangely enough I had started to become interested in Captain What's-His-Name Peachtree.

31

Wednesday morning I headed to the office bright and early like I promised Cal I would. He had beat me there as usual, and was typing away on his computer. Dora hadn't arrived yet.

"Morning, Cal," I hollered in the direction of his partition. No response, just the sound of his keyboard clacking.

"Sorry, Nola, I had to finish my thought," he answered once the clacking stopped.

"What are you working on?" I inquired as I sat down at my desk. Still no visual contact, but that wasn't unusual.

"Town council called a special meeting yesterday about bringing in a solar farm company to serve the community with electricity. Still in the planning stages, but may pan out in the future."

"Sounds great. We could use the publicity and the cheaper rates. Now, what do you want me working on since we only have today and tomorrow to finish up?"

"I could use some help with Page Three again," he suggested pleasantly. I noticed he sounded a lot more relaxed than I had ever known him to be.

"By the way, that finger the German tourists found turned out to be Tom Ballard's," I confirmed. "Or, at least that's what Doctor Barber surmised yesterday when I visited him in the hospital. He was the doctor who treated Tom after his accident with a chainsaw."

Cal finally came out from his cubicle. He appeared a lot spiffier than usual. "So that just leaves the hand as the most suspicious body part. And no word on that one yet. I'm leaving a small space open in case we get something, but I'm not going to worry about it."

Who was this? I wondered. Is this the same Cal I've always worked with? Or did he trade places with his alter-ego twin?

"What's come over you, Cal?" I pried. "You're not being your usual self today."

"I know. I haven't been myself since Monday. I asked Elsa Mae out on a date and she said 'yes.' We went to that new Mexican restaurant early Monday evening and had a great time. I've been wanting to ask her out for a long time, and I finally got up the courage. I think I'm in love, but I'm not sure, since I've never had a girlfriend before."

"Oh my gosh, Cal! How exciting!" That explained why he wasn't in the office that night and also the sudden change in his demeanor.

"We're going out again real soon. Gonna try Barney's Steakhouse this time. I've never been there before because I never had anyone to go with," he beamed.

"Well, I'm happy for you, Cal," I said and I meant it. "Now, let's get some work done, shall we?"

"We shall," he concurred as he walked jauntily back into his cubicle.

I liked this "new" Calvin Smythe. Maybe it was true that having someone special in your life made you a happier person. I guess I would have to find out for myself. Again.

I worked on Page Three, and then conferred with Cal on our progress. He was done with the front page and my awards bios were where he said they'd be—below the fold. His solar farm story, however, was *above* the fold. The photo was a stock one of another solar farm.

I had to wing it with Myrtle's bio, but I was able to put something together with what little Charlie had given me. I still wished I could have interviewed her instead.

Things seemed to be coming along smoothly, and we were ahead of schedule as far as deadline the next day was concerned. So, I offered to go check the police logs like Cal and I had talked about. He was more than happy to let me do that, even though he could have seen Elsa Mae at the police station. I guess he didn't want to appear too anxious. Besides, he knew they already had another date lined up.

Dora was arriving just as I was leaving.

"Afternoon shift?" I asked.

"Just for today. I had an appointment this morning."

"Well, I'm off to the police station," I informed her.

* * * *

The captain's car was once again parked in his assigned space. I took one of the empty visitor spots and went inside.

Elsa Mae was at her post, and was looking happier than ever. She'd had her short, brown hair touched up recently and had polished her nails. Evidently, her feeling was mutual with Cal's.

"Hi, Nola. What can I do for you this time?"

"I need to look at the police logs for the last few weeks, at least. Someone threw a rock through our office window last Thursday night, which should be noted in them, and Cal and I were wondering if we'd offended anyone recently in our reporting content."

"Sure. Hang on a second." She started to retrieve the logs when the phone rang. First things first. So I waited patiently.

I glanced up at the clock on the wall and saw that it was almost one o'clock by then. While I was wondering if Elsa Mae ever got to take a break, the door to the interior opened and Captain Peachtree emerged.

"Déjà vu. Here we are again," he joked.

"Captain. Good to see you too," I blushed.

"Is Elsa Mae helping you?" he asked.

"When she gets off the phone. She was getting me the recent police logs to look at when the phone rang."

"Can it wait? It's lunch time again. And this time you're going with me, because that's an order," he joked again.

"Well," I hesitated, "why not? I can check the logs when we get back. Where to, Captain?"

"Let's pick up some burgers and head to the park. How's that sound?"

"Lovely," was the first word that came to mind. Lovely? *Oh, my God, I think I like this guy more than I realized.*

He motioned to Elsa Mae, and then held the front door open for me to exit.

We drove in his official vehicle to the Burger Barn to pick up our meals, and then over to the community park. It was a beautiful fall day and there were several people enjoying strolls among the trees. We found an empty picnic table and he set our food bags and drinks down. We had both ordered the same things, so it didn't matter which was which.

Settling in across from each other with our burgers, fries and soft drinks, we resumed the conversation we were having in the car. Mainly, he'd asked me about my life in Northern California and what made me move back home.

I felt comfortable about being totally honest with him. Which had nothing to do with him being a cop—I didn't think. I liked him immediately, and sensed I could tell him anything without being judged. He kind of reminded me of Marty, but I quickly pushed that out of my head. No fair comparing him to my late husband.

He finished scarfing down his burger. "I'm sorry you lost your husband the way you did. Sounds like you guys had your whole future mapped out for you," he sympathized.

"Yeah, we thought we did. That's why it's always a good idea to live in the moment because you never know what tomorrow will bring. Wait. Did I just quote someone?" I took another bite out of my burger.

He laughed as he grabbed up a couple of French fries. "I don't know, but it sounds like good advice. I, on the other hand, am now divorced because my ex-wife didn't like living in this backwoods town when I was assigned here. She prefers the bustling city life. Turns out the divorce was a good thing because we had hardly anything in common anyway. Never had kids of our own, but she had two boys from her previous marriage which I helped raise. That is, until she packed them up and moved to the L.A. area."

"I'm sorry to hear that, but glad you're still here. By the way, I don't even know your first name. Some reporter that makes me, I know."

"Roger. Roger Allen Peachtree, at your service, ma'am."

I had just taken a sip of my soda and started choking with laughter. "Roger that, Captain. How appropriate." I continued clearing my throat.

"It gets better. My initials . . . R. A. P. . . . are appropriate also. As in 'rap sheet.' I must have been destined to become a cop from the moment I was born."

I laughed again. "So, where does the term 'rap' sheet come from, anyway?" I questioned.

"The word 'rap' itself goes back quite a few centuries to describe the sound of a knock on a door or a bang on the knuckles. In my line of work, it's said to represent the sound of a judge's gavel coming down when a person is declared guilty. Also used for 'bad rap' and 'bum rap' when the person feels he or she was judged unfairly. So, 'rap' sheet is a list of the guilty offenses. I guess the word would be considered an . . . ah-no-mah . . . something."

"Onomatopoeia. Like 'oink' or 'meow,' I think."

"You are very smart, Nola. That must be why I'm attracted to you."

"Are you? Well, you're smart enough yourself or else we wouldn't be having lunch together." I waved a French fry at him. "Now, what about the term 'rap' music? What does that mean?"

"I have no idea. I don't like it that much. I prefer country or classic rock myself."

"Me, too! Wow! Turns out we have a lot in common, don't we?" I remarked.

"Okay. Pop quiz. Lakers or Kings?" he started.

"Basketball? Ooh, that's a tough one. Being I was living up north, I was always a fan of the Kings. Now that I'm down here, however, I guess I'd better start rooting for the Lakers, or I might risk being ostracized."

"Good answer," he affirmed. "Your turn."

"Okay, let me think. Mmm, what did you want to be when you grew up?"

He didn't hesitate for a second before responding with, "A fireman. But I became a cop instead."

"Well, being a cop would still be considered a first responder, right?"

"Until you get stuck in an office. Not complaining. And what did you want to be?"

"A ballerina," I admitted sheepishly.

"A dancer? Can you? Dance, I mean?"

"Some, but I'm not very good at it. Okay, you go again," I suggested.

"Okay, what's your favorite movie?"

"You'll have to narrow that down a bit," I suggested.

"Classic film then."

"I love *The Wizard of Oz*."

"Mine would be *Citizen Kane*, I think."

"So, what's your favorite color?" is what he came up with.

"Purple . . . all shades," I answered right away.

"Mine is navy blue," he revealed.

"Purple and navy blue kinda go together. They're in the same color spectrum, right? So there's another connection," I offered.

"I know one when I see one," he winked at me. He then glanced at his watch. "Time to get back. I wish we could stay longer. You are extremely enjoyable, Nola."

I didn't know how to respond to that, so I just smiled sweetly and said, "Thanks, Roger."

32

Back at the office, Dora was still on duty since she had come in late that day. She handed me a bunch of display ads that needed to be placed, and then returned to typing up the news briefs.

I told Cal that I had checked the police logs and didn't find anything suspicious. He, in turn, directed me as to which pages the ads should go.

Once situated at my desk, I began my assigned task, but I was having trouble concentrating.

I was still reeling from my lunch with Roger. Realizing I was starting to like him more and more scared me. I hadn't told Cal about the lunch, not wanting to upstage his new romance. I *did* tell him that Elsa Mae was looking great, however. That made him grin from ear to ear.

Several hours had gone by before I decided to call it a day. I told Cal I'd see him first thing in the morning and headed on home.

I performed my standard evening routine on automatic pilot. I still couldn't get Roger out of my head. Darn him!

I talked to Pinky briefly to let her know I had taken her advice and had lunch with Captain Peachtree. I informed her that from now on he will be referred to as *Roger*. She was thrilled and proud of me. Baby steps, I told her, baby steps.

I wasn't that hungry, but I ate something anyway, and then took a glass of wine out to the front porch to sit and watch the bats flitting about scarfing up insects. It was almost dusk—or what I like to refer to as Bat:30. Their nightly show would only continue for another month or so before they went into hibernation, so I tried not to miss one.

I had always wanted to be a bird in my next life. But now I think I want to be a bat. Bats are sorely misunderstood and maligned creatures. They serve a useful purpose in nature's scheme of things, for heaven's sake. Plus, they get to sleep a lot.

I sat there pondering the hedonistic life of a bat, and counting how many of them I could spot as the twilight began fading fast. I was jolted out of my reverie when I heard my house phone ring through the open window.

I had been feeling so relaxed that I almost ignored the incoming call. But it was probably Mother, so I went inside to answer.

It wasn't Mother. It was Roger.

"Hi, Nola. I just wanted to tell you what a great time I had with you today. We really should get together more often. How about sometime this weekend?"

"Well, I have to attend the community awards dinner on Saturday. Maybe Sunday?"

"I'll be at the awards dinner also. But Sunday is perfect. Harold Raymond is having a barbecue that afternoon in honor of Cecil Barber and I was invited. Wanna go with?" Roger asked.

How strange that the MJ club would invite the police captain to their party. But if they did, I thought, then they must not be worried about him knowing about their activities. Hmmm. The lack of paranoia might open up the chance to observe all the members, including Dr. Barber.

"Can we bring my mom?" I thought having a buffer might give me more time to think about this sudden attraction.

"Sure. I have yet to meet her. So it's a date," he confirmed with a smile in his voice.

"Okay. What time?"

"Harold said the barbecue will start around four. I'll pick you up about three-thirty so we'll have time to go fetch Mom," he affirmed intimately.

"You know where my house is?"

"Of course. That historic one on Oak Street. One of the nicest older homes in Cider Crossing."

"I think so, too," I responded. "Hey, are there any new developments in the missing Myrtle Maxwell case?"

"Jeff talked to Mac Donovan and was told that she had dropped off her car a week ago Friday morning and then walked home. She was supposed to pick it up first thing Monday morning, but she never showed. That tells me she must have gone missing sometime over that weekend—from Friday to Monday morning. That's all we got."

"Strange. And the detectives? Have they come up with anything?"

"They've interviewed everyone close to her, and now they're circling outward. Anyone she knows or interacts with."

"Sheesh! That could be a lot. What about the hand? Any word from the lab yet?"

"Well, I told you that they said it was probably removed with a saw. They also said the missing finger appears to have been *pulled* off, not sawn. You know, like dislocated. I know that doesn't help much. We really need to get some DNA results or something more definitive."

"I agree. Okay, see you on Sunday." I was about to hang up when he continued.

"Wait. Let me give you my cell number in case something comes up," he offered.

He rattled off the number, which I was scratching down on a post-it when I heard the familiar *beep* of an incoming call.

"I have to take this call, Roger. Bye," I said hurriedly before switching over. Once again, I was assuming it would be Mother. It wasn't. It was Florence.

"Florence. How are you?" I asked, trying to sound as pleasant as possible.

"Nola. You won't believe this. I had been watering and rearranging all the floral displays at the clubhouse when Iris's rose bush fell off the table. The pot broke into pieces, and when I was cleaning up the mess I discovered a finger caught up in the root system. This is weird. What should I do?" She sounded out of breath.

"Don't touch anything. Leave it right where it is. And call the police department to report this, Florence. It may be the missing finger from that hand that showed up mysteriously the other day. Meanwhile, I'll head over to talk to Iris at her house."

"I'll do that, Nola, but be careful. Heaven knows what she's been up to," Florence speculated in her accusatory fashion.

Even though Iris lived close by, I decided to drive over there. I grabbed my cell phone off its charger, and the post-it with Roger's number on it, and stuffed them both into my purse. I had changed into sweatpants when I got home, so I donned the matching jacket and then headed out to my car.

As soon as I came upon the Pettis house, I could tell there were no lights on at all—not even the porch light. The place was as dark as a tomb. Bert's red pickup was parked on the driveway, however. Which meant that Iris must be home, right? Or not. Maybe she was back to driving her own car.

Puzzled by what I was observing, I decided to take a drive down Main Street to see if Iris was out and about.

33

I used to listen to country music all the time, either at home or in the car. That genre seemed to fit in well with the environment in which I was living at the time—the gold country in Northern California. But since I had moved back home, the only radio station that came in clearly that I could relate to was the one that featured classic rock. Which was fine with me, since, as I had told Roger, I enjoy that era also. I do miss the country, though.

With the radio turned down low, I started at one end of Main Street and began cruising at a slow pace while scoping out all the establishments along the way to see if I could spot the car Iris must have been driving—her silver Subaru.

Most of the businesses were closed for the night. Near the ones that were still open, I could see no Subaru parked out front.

As foreboding as it turned out, I could hear Electric Light Orchestra's "Evil Woman" started playing on the car radio as I approached Bert's Butcher Shop. I turned up the volume a little and began to sing along.

"There's a hole in my head where the rain comes in . . ."

There were a few cars parked along the curb in front of Ernie's Liquor Store next door to Bert's, but, once again, no Subaru. Drat! Where the hell can she be? I wondered.

"But you ain't got nobody else to blame . . ."

Right away I noticed a faint light glowing in the rear of the butcher shop as I passed by. I kept on driving, but hung a right at the next street to approach again from the alleyway.

"Evil Woman" continued playing as I crept into the alley. The first thing I noticed up ahead in my headlights was the rear end of a silver Subaru parked behind the butcher shop. Aha!

I stopped a few yards back, carefully got out of my car, locked my purse inside and put the keys inside a pocket.

I then tip-toed up to the vehicle and slowly made my way around to the front end. I didn't have a flashlight on me, so all I had were a couple of street lamps lighting up the alleyway. But that was enough illumination to expose the damage to the front right bumper of Iris' car. Smashed in. Headlight broken. Interesting.

Suddenly convinced that it must have been Iris who ran Dr. Barber off the road, I wondered what her motive could have been. Nothing immediately came to mind.

Assuming Iris was inside the shop, I stealthily made my way up to the back door to listen for any sign that I was correct. The door was slightly cracked open, but not locked as I would have expected. I put my ear next to the opening. Nothing. But I did detect the unmistakable odor of bleach wafting out into the alleyway.

ELO's lyrics were still bouncing around inside my head as I gently pushed open the door.

"*Ha, ha, woman, what you gonna do,*" Jeff Lynne sang to me. Or was he singing that to Iris?

34

Peering inside, I could see where the light had been coming from. The door to what appeared to be the walk-in cold storage locker was slightly ajar, casting the glow that I had noticed earlier.

There was just enough illumination for me to tell that Iris was nowhere in the outer part of the narrow shop. That told me she must be inside the locker. I went on in.

The bleach smell got stronger as I moved toward the open door. So far, so good. I assumed she must not be able to hear me from behind the thick walls.

I cautiously peered inside. The view was restricted, but I felt no coldness emanating from within, so I assumed the refrigeration had been shut off.

I could barely see Iris, dressed in a T-shirt, jeans and tennis shoes, crouched down on the floor with her bleach and paper towels, scrubbing away.

There were no creepy animal carcasses hanging from the ceiling, but what frightened me the most was the pair of feet wearing canvas espadrilles which I could see when I looked down. The rest of the body was blocked from my sight, but I was positive that it must be Myrtle's.

I should have shut the door on Iris right then, but I knew I would have to block her in while I called for help. But how? I looked around for something to barricade the door with. Unfortunately, that took too long.

Iris had seen me and had bolted out of the cold storage, slamming the door behind her. She headed straight for me. I turned to get away but she reached out and grabbed me by the hair, all the time yelling, "What are you doing here? What are you doing here?"

I swung around and tried knock her down. That didn't work. I looked around for something to hit her with, but she had grabbed a meat cleaver off a rack and was swinging it at me. "Get out, get out! Or I'll kill you."

"Iris, put the cleaver down," I ordered.

"You have no business being in here," she snapped angrily. Apparently, she was unaware of what I had seen.

"Iris, I saw the body. I saw Myrtle's body," I ventured. "You can't get away with this."

"Stupid, stupid old bitch. Sneaking around with my Bert. Having her way with him. She deserved what she got." She was still waving the cleaver around.

"What the heck are you talking about, Iris?" I was perplexed.

"I found the letters—the *love* letters. When I was going through Bert's things. They're on the front counter in a shoe box. I'm going to destroy them. 'Dear B' she called him. Nothing but a cheap whore, I say."

"Those letters weren't sent to Bert. Those were the love letters Myrtle had sent to Greg Goldberg when he was stationed in Okinawa," I corrected her, hoping she would give in to reason.

"Yeah, right. I don't believe that. Besides, why would Bert have them? They were doing it, alright. Can't fool me."

"You're not thinking straight, Iris. Greg's nickname is Buddy, remember? He had given them to Bert for safe keeping when he married his wife. And the letters, without envelopes, probably weren't dated. So, you mistakenly assumed they were recent. See?" I was trying to reason with her again, but it wasn't working.

"I'm not stupid and I don't make mistakes," she bragged. "You shoulda stayed out of this. I warned you, Nola. Now, I have to take care of you, too," she growled.

Ignoring her threat, I asked, "So, you're the one who threw the rock through my office window? That was you?"

"Damn right. I told you to 'back off' but you wouldn't listen. Then, I thought I ran you off the road, but it was Cecil instead. Damn!" She had begun to move backwards toward an old band saw table Bert must have used to cut meat.

"You're an Evil Woman, Iris," I dished out the perfect insult, thanks to ELO.

That got her dander up. "How dare you!" she hollered as she reached back and switched on the band saw. Its vertical blade started whirring up and down.

"So, is that the weapon you used to kill Myrtle?" I asked loud enough to compete with the band saw motor.

"It was an accident!" she shrieked. "Not murder! I yanked her out of her house and brought her over here to have it out with her, that's all. She kept on denying she'd been having an affair with my late husband, the little harlot.

"We kept on arguing and I pushed her toward the saw table. She hit the switch when she bumped up against it. So I pushed her again and her wrist hit the blade. The saw didn't completely sever it, so I had to finish the job.

"Fortunately, she was bleeding to death by then, anyway. And dripping blood all over the floor. Damn her."

I could tell she felt absolutely no remorse for what she had done, so I knew she'd tell me more. "What did you do with the hand?"

"Buried it in my garden, under a rose bush. But then some mongrel dog dug it up and carried it off before I could stop it. Stupid dog. I hate dogs," she added with disgust.

"And what do you plan to do with the rest of her body?" I inquired out of curiosity.

"I haven't decided yet. I thought of running her piece-by-piece through the meat grinder, but that would be too much work and too messy striping the flesh off the bones. Maybe I'll just chop her up and toss the pieces in the dumpster. Or maybe burn the pieces in my fireplace," she chuckled. "Don't know yet. But at least I've gotten most of the cleaning done around here. There won't be any evidence left when I'm through."

"You're never going to get away with this, Iris," I predicted.

"Of course I will, because you're going to help me get her into the trunk of my car," she replied smugly. "I've got the tarp all ready," she added.

"I would *never* help you do such a despicable thing," I refuted.

A demonic look flashed over her face. "Well then," she snarled, "I'll simply have to deal with you first."

With that last statement, she raised the cleaver above her head and came charging at me.

35

I frantically high-tailed it to the back door. But Iris was right behind me. She swung the cleaver at me just as I ducked down. The cleaver sliced into the wooden door and got wedged there.

As she was struggling to dislodge her weapon, I turned and ran to the front door. It was key-locked. Damn. What to do?

I spotted several knives hanging from the same rack where the cleaver had been, but I couldn't get to them in time. Iris had wrestled the cleaver out of the back door and was heading right back at me.

The band saw was still in motion. I needed to turn it off. But, in my panic, I couldn't see where the switch was located. Besides, Iris had almost reached me by then. I got behind the band saw table to block her attack.

As she was coming at me, still wielding the cleaver, I shoved the heavy table toward her. She lost her balance and her lower left arm flew right into the vibrating saw blade. The cleaver went flying past my head.

Iris fell to the floor and began screaming. Her arm was bleeding profusely, but it didn't appear to be severed.

I looked around for something to staunch the bleeding. On the front counter I spotted the butcher paper roll and a spool of twine. I ripped off a wad of paper and grabbed the twine off its post.

The functioning band saw came in handy when I pulled out a length of twine and used the saw to cut it. I quickly tied the twine around her upper arm and pushed the paper into the wound. Iris had stopped screaming, but she had begun moaning.

"Iris. You need to hold the paper in place while I call for help. Where's the phone?" I yelled.

"Aaaahhhggg!" Iris hollered as she pushed down on the butcher paper with her right hand.

I went back to the front counter to search for the phone. When I found it, I picked up the receiver only to hear nothing. No dial tone. Dammit!

On my way back to Iris, I noticed where the saw was plugged in. I yanked the saw's power cord out of its socket. The sudden silence was deafening.

"Keep pressing down hard. I'm going to go get my phone," I told her.

I headed to the back door and flung it open. As I stepped out into the alley, the back door to the liquor store opened and Carol, Jeff's wife, came out.

"What's going on? I thought I heard someone scream," Carol said.

I was reaching into my right pants pocket for my car keys, but couldn't feel them.

"Call 9-1-1," I shrieked. "Iris is injured." I didn't want to tell her that her boss was also lying dead on the cold storage floor.

Carol quickly ducked back inside, while I kept digging through my pockets. I finally found the keys in my jacket pocket and went running to my car.

Snatching my purse off the passenger seat, I fumbled inside it for my phone and the post-it with Roger's cell number on it.

"Roger. Butcher shop. STAT!" I rapid-fired as soon as he answered.

"Already on my way."

36

It didn't take long for the paramedics to show up. And Roger was right behind them, along with several other officers. Good thing I had unlocked the front door with the shop keys Iris had told me where to find, so no one would have to bash in the glass.

While the responders were working on Iris, I took Roger back to the cold storage so he could see where Myrtle had ended up.

It was a sad sight to see. We both stood there in the open cold storage doorway without saying a word. Myrtle appeared to be sleeping. Except for the fact that she was missing her left hand, she seemed somewhat normal.

"Crime scene and the detectives are on their way," Roger told me. "The coroner's van is on its way, too."

I related everything Iris had told me about what had happened. Her suspicions about Bert and Myrtle having an affair. What a shame. A woman had died because of a misunderstanding.

"That reminds me, Iris said the love letters were in a shoe box on the front counter. They might be some kind of evidence to prove motive, or something."

"Great. I'll let the forensic team know," he said.

"Even though Iris claims it was an accident, she didn't call for help, so I blame her for Myrtle's death," I declared.

"That'll be up to the jury to decide," Roger stated. "But I agree with you. And you'll probably have to testify to her confession."

"I don't mind, as long as it gets her locked up for good. She's a nut job, in my opinion."

"I'm just glad you're okay," Roger confessed. "She could have killed you, too."

"Nah. I wouldn't let her," I replied in my cocky fashion.

He stood there in his civilian clothes looking as handsome as ever with an adoring smile on his face. I have to admit, it gave me butterflies. At a crime scene, no less.

"So, what's next?" I continued, trying not to be distracted.

"Well, they'll have to get her the proper medical attention, but she will be under arrest. Meanwhile, the CSI's will have to do their thing, and then they'll release the body to the coroner's office. All in a day's work," Roger affirmed.

"And what about me?" I questioned.

"The detectives will have to take a statement from you—probably tomorrow."

"Then, can I go now? I mean, I want to help, but I'm exhausted," I realized, as a wave of weariness suddenly came over me.

"Sure. I'll walk you out to your car," Roger offered.

As we stood in the alley by my car, saying our good-byes, Roger reached out and gave me a big hug. The hug was followed by a kiss—and not just a peck—a long, passionate one. It almost took what was left of my breath away.

"You've made my world whole again, Nola," Roger proclaimed, and then he immediately turned on his heels and went back into the butcher shop.

He left me speechless. I don't know how long I stood there, staring off into space, but I finally got into my car and drove myself home.

37

Bright and early the next morning, I rushed through my usual routine and headed straight for the office. Cal's car was already parked in the front lot along with Dora's.

"Stop the presses!" I blasted out as I burst through the front door.

"What?" Dora and Cal called out simultaneously.

"Myrtle Maxwell's killer has been arrested," I reported unceremoniously.

Cal came out from behind his partition. "Myrtle is dead? Who did it?"

"Iris did. Iris Pettis. So we have a big story to tell. Let's get to it," I ordered as I made my way to my cubicle.

"That's awful," said Dora. "I always liked Myrtle. I got my new puppy from her rescue shelter."

"I know. And it was so unnecessary. A complete misunderstanding. And now Myrtle is gone," I sighed.

I went on to tell them the complete story from beginning to end.

"Well, this breaking news trumps the solar farm story. We'll have to move that one to another page because this tragedy gets top billing," Cal declared.

"And I need to talk to Florence so I can edit my fall flower show story. I'm pretty sure she'll be removing Iris from the competition winners."

"Good idea, Nola."

"Do you want *me* to write the Myrtle story, or do *you*?" I asked Cal.

"Being you were sorta involved in her apprehension, I think it's best if I write it—from a more objective point of view, you understand."

"Of course. You can check with Roger . . . I mean . . . Captain Peachtree, to get all the details."

"Calling him 'Roger' now, are we?" Cal teased.

Dora was giggling away while typing.

"You're not the only one with a potential paramour, Cal," I retorted.

"*Touché*, Nola."

I had been taken so far out of my comfort zone by Roger, that I had forgotten there were several people I needed to share the sad news with: Mother, Buddy and Pinky. But who first?

Both Mother and Buddy would be devastated, so Pinky could wait. And I was pretty sure that Myrtle's next of kin had already been notified, so I'd better call Mother first before the town's grapevine reached her.

"Mom?" I started when she answered.

"Nola? It's so early, dear. Why are you calling me?" That question told me she was still unaware of what happened.

"Mom. I have some bad news. Myrtle's been found."

But before I could continue, Mother blurted out, "Isn't that good news, Nola?"

"No, Mom, she was found dead."

"Dead? Oh my goodness! What happened?" Lillian started sniffling.

"It's a long story, but basically Iris Pettis is responsible. I discovered Myrtle's body at Bert's Butcher Shop. Iris was there cleaning up and she tried to do me in, too. Fortunately, help arrived and they've arrested her. Anyway, I've got several other calls to make, so I'll come by later to make sure you're okay, okay?"

"Yes, dear. Oh, how terrible. I need to call Olive, or Winnie, or Nellie, or . . ."

"Okay, Mom, see you later," I said before hanging up.

My next call was to Buddy. Since his cell number was already in my cell, I used my own phone instead of the office phone, and stepped outside for privacy.

"I heard, Nola," was the first thing out of Buddy's mouth when he answered.

"How?" I was surprised how fast the news had traveled.

"Ivy told me. She's still in shock. Local law enforcement had paid her a notification visit last night and she called me first thing this morning. Such a tragedy, and we still don't have all the details," I could hear him blow his nose. "I'm feeling rather numb right now."

"I'm so, so sorry, Buddy. I know how much you cared for her," I sympathized.

"Do you know how it happened?" he asked.

"Strangely enough, Iris confessed everything to me," I started, and then hesitated. I wasn't sure if I should tell him about the role the letters had played. But, then again, if they were put into evidence, he would find out anyway. So I decided to lay it all out.

"Nola? Are you still there?" Buddy asked.

"Sorry. I was trying to get everything straight in my head. Please, try not to get too upset by what I'm about to tell you," I cautioned.

"Just tell me," he urged.

"Okay, so Iris told me that she had forced Myrtle to go to the butcher shop. There she accused her of having an affair with Bert."

"What made her think that?" he questioned.

"Well, she had been going through Bert's things after he died, and she came across the letters you had given him for safe keeping."

"I don't get the connection," Buddy interrupted.

"She thought the 'B' was for Bert," I explained.

"But I'm sure Myrtle told her they were written to me."

"I'm sure she did, but Iris didn't believe her. She didn't believe me either. She was hell-bent on condemning Myrtle for messing around with her husband. Obviously, she's not all there."

"Oh my God! It's all my fault!" Buddy cried.

"Buddy, how can it be your fault? Iris is looney. This is all on her, not you."

"But if I hadn't given Bert the letters, none of this would have happened."

"Life is full of 'what-ifs' we can't change."

"I still feel awful. And I still don't know how she died."

I decided to cut right to the chase. "Iris pushed her into the running band saw and she bled to death." I didn't want to get into the minute details.

"Oh, no! I thought maybe Iris hit her over the head or something. Not that!" He then started to cry.

"Oh, Buddy, I wish I was there to comfort you," was all I could think to say.

"When can I get the letters back? They're all I have to remember her by," was his next thought.

"They might have to be used to prove motive during the trial, so it may be a while. But I'll check and see what I can find out and let you know, okay?"

"Oh, my God! I'll never see her again."

"She'll always be with you, Buddy. I know what it's like to lose someone. I lost my husband over two years ago. But I still feel his presence every once in a while."

"I'm so glad you're there, Nola. You've been a big help, even though this didn't have a happy ending."

"I know. I'll talk to you soon. Take care."

38

As soon as I hung up from consoling Buddy, and returned to my desk, I remembered I needed to get in touch with Florence. I tried calling her at home, but got no answer. She must be at the botanical society clubhouse getting ready for the awards ceremony, I assumed. I would have to drive over there.

As I was gathering up my things, the office door opened and in stepped two well-dressed gentlemen. I pegged them as the detectives right away.

"We're here to speak with Nola Martin," one of them told Dora.

"Right here," I informed them. I put my stuff down as they approached.

"Detective Evans, and this is Detective Ramirez," he introduced. "Is there somewhere we can talk?"

"Let's go into the editor's office," I suggested. He's on vacation."

I seated myself behind Julius' desk and began to repeat my account of what happened for what seemed like the tenth time. From their guest seats, they both took copious notes and asked a multitude of questions.

"Greg Goldberg, also known as Buddy, was the actual recipient of the letters. He would like to know when he can get them back," I informed them.

"They'll be used to establish motive, I'm sure," said Detective Evans as he scribbled in his notebook. "But we can return them to him after the trial."

"Someone told us he lives in Dowd. Is that correct?" asked Detective Ramirez. "We should interview him also. Put all the pieces together."

"Yes, he lives in Dowd. His home number is listed in the Dowd phone book."

Ramirez nodded and made a note.

I was beginning to think the interview would never end, and I had become weary of the whole thing, when they stood up together and thanked me for my time. Finally.

* * * *

After the detectives left the office, I drove over to the botanical society. Sure enough, Florence was bustling about getting the place ready for the ribbon awards scheduled for that afternoon.

"Hi, Florence. I'm sure you heard about Myrtle by now," I greeted her morbidly.

"Yes, I heard. That must have been her finger I found. Even though I didn't like her that much, I think it's awful what Iris did to her."

"Me, too. My goodness, news sure travels fast around here." I looked around the room and saw a container of yellow hibiscus flowers.

"Are those Myrtle's hibiscus?"

"Yes, they are. Winnie and Olive have been keeping up with the outside watering at Myrtle's house. Charlie wouldn't let them have a key to take care of anything inside the house. Anyway, Winnie cut those flowers and brought them here this morning. We decided that Myrtle should get an honorable mention today."

"That's very nice of all of you," I commended as I snapped some pics.

"Least we can do."

"I think it's a great idea. Now, I need an update on any changes in the ribbon recipients due to this tragedy."

"So, Iris has been removed from the ribbon winners list and Peggy Jacobs will get the ribbon instead. She was right behind Iris in votes. That's her entry over there," she motioned toward a vase of coral roses at the end of the display table.

"Peggy Jacobs, right. Let me take a few photos of her flowers and then I'll be on my way. I won't be back for the gathering because we've gotta make deadline this afternoon. But the story will be in tomorrow's edition."

39

As I drove back to the office, I reminded myself that I still had to call Pinky with the news. I'd rather do that in the comfort of my own home, however, so I forged on to getting the paper put to bed first.

Cal was just getting off the phone when I came in. "Nola? Is that you?" he inquired from behind his partition.

"How's the story coming, Cal?"

"I think I've got everything I need. Just finished talking to Captain Peachtree, so I'm gonna start writing up the copy now. I'll have you look at it when I'm done."

"What do you need me to do?"

Cal rattled off a few assignments as I settled in to complete them. I needed to edit my flower show story first. It was going to be sad.

Several hours later, I had finished up the last task Cal had given me when he asked me to bring up the murder story to read over for him.

Well written, in typical Calvin style, it almost brought me to tears.

"Great job, Cal. You got all the details correct. Are we ready to transmit yet?"

"I need to go over all the pages one last time, but if you want to go home and get some rest, I understand."

"Thanks, Cal. I do need to recuperate from all this. It has been rather draining."

"Well, *git* on home then," he ordered as he returned to his desk.

I closed down my computer and grabbed what I needed to take home with me. As I shuffled past the front desk, I realized I hadn't even noticed that Dora had left for the day. I guess she didn't want to disturb us with her good-byes.

* * * *

I stopped by Mother's house to check on her like I said I would, and then I headed to my place. Once back home, I told myself I needed to eat something. I was feeling weak, and maybe that was why. So I snatched a few leftovers out of the fridge and ate them standing up at the kitchen counter. I then poured myself a glass of iced tea, picked up the house phone and headed out to the front porch to call Pinky.

"Sad news, Pinky," I reported as soon as she answered.

"Oh, no, Nola. What happened?"

"Myrtle's dead. Iris did it. I almost got whacked also."

"What? How? When?"

"You left out Where and Why."

"You're the reporter not me, smartass. Okay, spill it all."

I repeated the story for the umpteenth time, but this time I didn't leave out any details. I knew Pinky could handle all the blood and gore.

"Sheesh! What an ordeal. I'm just glad you made it out safely. It could have turned out differently."

"Don't I know that. I literally had to think on my feet. I still don't know how I was able to push that heavy band saw toward her. Must have been an adrenaline rush is all I can figure," I posited.

"You're probably right. I've heard some amazing stories about people doing that. Anyway, so she's going to be locked up and, hopefully, the key will be thrown far away."

"Well, she will have to stand trial, but I don't see her getting away with murder."

"I feel bad for Buddy. After all, it was sort of a new beginning for both of them," Pinky romanticized.

"Speaking of new beginnings, I have some juicy gossip on that front. About myself, of all people."

"What? Juicy? What have you been up to, Nola? Is it about Captain Peachtree—excuse me, Roger?"

"Yes, it's about Roger. He has been growing on me, despite my tendency to resist male attention."

"Okay, go on, let me in on all the wicked details."

"He kissed me. There. I said it."

"Alright! When did that happen?"

"Right after my confrontation with Iris. After it was over, and all the first responders had arrived, he walked me out to my car. He told me he was relieved

I wasn't injured, and then he hugged me. The hug evolved into a nice, long kiss."

"I'm impressed, Nola."

"He also said I had made his world whole again, or something like that. I don't know, I was stunned at the time."

"Progress. What's next?"

"Well, we're going to attend a barbecue at Harold Raymond's on Sunday, and we're taking Mother with us. The pot club is honoring Doctor Barber's recovery. But before that, on Saturday night we'll both be attending the community awards dinner. Only I'll be in my usual work mode while covering the event."

"Isn't it odd that the police captain is hobnobbing with the MJ crew?"

"I thought the same thing myself. Maybe he's not aware? I find that hard to believe, however. Oh, well, this should be interesting."

"I'm so glad you found someone, Nola. You deserve to be happy again."

"Not so fast. It's all so new. But I do have to admit that he gives me the butterflies," I giggled.

40

"**Prominent local citizen found dead**" was the top story in Friday's edition of the Cider Press, and it was a major sensation. The glaring headline and story was all that people were talking about around town. My article about the flower show didn't receive nearly as much attention, although people were pleased that Myrtle had received the honorable mention for her hibiscus.

I had tried to contact Charlie to offer my condolences, but he wasn't talking to anyone. Blanche had answered the phone and had informed me of this. She also told me that Myrtle's funeral would be held the following week, but the exact day was yet to be determined. I asked her to e-mail me an obituary, which she said she would as soon as she had more information.

I also thought of calling Ivy, but I called Buddy instead.

"How's Ivy doing?" I asked him.

"As well as can be expected, I guess. At least we have each other to talk to. She hasn't even talked to her brother yet. What a depressing situation," he sighed.

"How's your wife doing?" I asked.

"Well, she is totally unaware of my connection to Myrtle, but I told her that someone from my hometown that I went to school with had been murdered. She was sympathetic. As far as her health is concerned, she's been pretty stable. I just wish she could be cured altogether, but I guess that's not in the cards."

"I'm sorry, Buddy. You both deserve to be happy." We *all* do, I added to myself.

"I'm doing my best to make sure the rest of her life is stress-free and pleasant. I *do* love her, you know," he confirmed.

"I know you do. Well, if there is anything I can do for you, just let me know. And let's keep in touch, okay?"

"Sure, Nola, you've been a godsend already."

41

Saturday night's community awards dinner at the Moose Lodge was bittersweet. It was great to see worthy people being honored for their contributions to the town, but it was sad that one of them was no longer with us.

Betty Rayburn was awarded Business of the Year, even though she ran a non-profit. Joe Dana was awarded Volunteer of the Year for his dedication to promoting youth sports. Margaret Sampson was awarded Educator of the Year for furthering education through her scholarship program. And last, but not least, Myrtle Maxwell was posthumously awarded Citizen of the Year.

Charlie didn't attend the function, but Blanche was there to accept the award on Myrtle's behalf.

Of course, Roger and I ended up sitting together at a table with some other law enforcement members, while I took notes and pictures. Calvin was on another date with Elsa Mae. I had brought Mother with me, but she was sitting with some of her church friends. I had been able to introduce her to Roger when we first arrived, however.

I was hoping no one at our table had picked up on the obvious attraction between Roger and me, but Jeff kept smiling and winking at me. He'd better keep his mouth shut, I thought. At least for now.

The dinner had been rather subdued, and no one hung around for very long afterward. Since Roger and I had arrived separately, we were leaving separately. He reminded me he would be picking me up the following afternoon to attend the barbecue.

He walked me and Mother out to my car, gave us both hugs, but no kisses this time. Obviously.

On the ride to Mother's house, she intuitively stated that Roger seemed definitely interested in me and that she hoped it would work out.

"It's about time you found someone, Nola. You're young enough to start a whole new phase of your life. I, on the other hand, am too old to start over. Your dad was the love of my life and always will be."

"I don't know, Mom. You never know when love might be waiting just around the corner," I teased.

"Oh, good night!"

42

Roger arrived to pick me up promptly at 3:30 as he said he would. Handsome as usual in a western shirt and boots this time.

I invited him in for a brief tour of the remodel. He was duly impressed with everything I had done so far, but he was especially impressed with the old-fashioned looking, but totally modernized, cook stove I had installed in the kitchen. Its era pre-dated the founding of the town, but I didn't care. I liked it, and so did he. Turns out he loves to cook. Who woulda thunk?

As we were heading over to pick up Mother, Roger turned to me and said, "I have a confession to make."

Oh, no, I thought. Where is he going with this? But I calmly replied, "Okay, hit me with it."

"I have a CCTV screen in my office. For security purposes, you understand. But that's how I always knew when you were out in the lobby at the station. I looked forward to seeing you every time you showed up. I even invited you to lunch one time when I had just finished eating my lunch at my desk. That's how much I wanted to spend time with you. I'm smitten, Nola. I'm just hoping you feel the same. There. I'm done with my confession."

"Oh, my, Roger. I didn't expect that. But I have to admit that my feelings for you have been steadily growing. Maybe not as fast as yours, but I am definitely attracted to you. I just need more time to catch up with where you're at. Something tells me it won't be long, however."

* * * *

The barbecue was in full swing when the three of us arrived. Mother immediately went to chat with Nellie. Olive and Winnie were swinging on the hammock. Archie was helping out in the kitchen and Harold was tending to his new grill.

After Roger deposited the case of Stella Artois he had brought to the party, we both approached Cecil to welcome him back home and to let him know that we were glad he was okay. He exclaimed he was totally shocked that it was Iris who had run him off the road.

Country music was playing and Roger asked me to line dance to "Boot Scootin' Boogie" with him. We ended up laughing so hard because we couldn't get the steps right, and so we finally gave up.

We filled our paper plates with food, grabbed some drinks and sat at one of two picnic tables Harold had in his backyard.

I was having more fun than I had in ages. And I soon realized I was falling in love with Roger.

I was still curious about one question, however: How was it that he was socializing with people who were technically breaking the law? So, I leaned forward and asked him about that in a lowered voice.

He covered one eye with his right hand and winked the other one.

"What does that mean?" I asked

"It means I'm turning a blind eye," he explained.

"To the MJ club?" I couldn't help being specific.

"The stuff is going to be legal here any time now, anyway. And it's not like they're in business to peddle it. So, all for the greater good, I say. Doctor Barber has helped improve the lives of people who would have otherwise been miserable. I say more power to him." And then he added, "But don't repeat that."

"My lips are sealed," I promised.

"I sure hope not. I *love* French kissing," he laughed uproariously.

Once again, he left me speechless. I just grinned.

Mother was ready to leave right after she ate, so she came to tell us that Nellie was driving her home.

"Stay and enjoy yourself, Nola," she urged. "You've earned it." She then turned to Roger and said, "Hope to see you again real soon, Captain."

Roger and I decided to try dancing again after we were finished with our plates. We were much better at waltzing to the slow songs, but the intimacy of cheek-to-cheek was becoming somewhat stimulating for the both of us. George Strait wasn't helping much either, by crooning "You Look So Good in Love."

"Shall we?" he whispered in my ear.

"Shall we what?" I cross-questioned with a rapidly beating heart.

"Go back to your place?"

"Roger that . . . uh . . . Roger," I uttered, trying to sound as nonchalant as I possibly could.

ABOUT THE AUTHOR

Marjorie Dario is a retired state employee living in a tri-state area near the Colorado River. She and her three cats enjoy a slow-paced lifestyle allowing *her* to pursue her writing and for *them* to pursue their napping. Upon moving to the area from Sacramento, she spent three years as a reporter/photographer for the *Needles Desert Star*. She is currently working on her third Nola Martin Mystery.

CPSIA information can be obtained
at www.ICGtesting.com
Printed in the USA
LVHW041321071019
633401LV00004B/574/P

9 781796 611625